IN DEEP DARK WOOD

'An enchanting story with a magical touch'
Southside People

'An absorbing tale of magic and dragons by one
of our most popular children's writers'
Sunday Independent

'You will have to read this enchanting book.
And as you read, you will find yourself falling
under the spell of Conlon-McKenna's
wonderful writing and vivid imagination'
Dublin Echo

In deep dark wood the old woman stirred. All day long the noise had continued, the buzzing of huge saws, the rolling thunder of heavy yellow machines, and the ominous creak and roar as tree after tree fell – oak, chestnut and ash, all crashing to the torn earth below.

Hiding herself amongst the leaves she watched the men working. The time had come. She must care for and protect her treasures, move them. Her old bones ached and her head was addled thinking of it, but even she knew that it was century's end and soon she must be gone ...

In Deep
Dark Wood

Marita Conlon-McKenna

THE O'BRIEN PRESS
DUBLIN

For Fiona and James – my heroes

First published 1999 by The O'Brien Press Ltd,
12 Terenure Road East, Rathgar, Dublin 6, Ireland.
Tel: +353 1 4923333; Fax: +353 1 4922777
E-mail: books@obrien.ie
Website: www.obrien.ie
Reprinted 1999, 2001, 2002, 2005 (twice), 2007, 2009, 2011, 2012.

ISBN 978-0-86278-615-1

A catalogue record for this title is available from
The British Library

10 11 12
12 13 14 15

Typesetting, layout, editing and design: The O'Brien Press Ltd
Printed and bound by CPI Group (UK) Ltd, Croydon, CR0 4YY
The paper used in this book is produced using pulp from
managed forests

The O'Brien Press receives assistance from

CONTENTS

Chapter 1

Stormy Winds

The wild west wind gathered its strength out over the Atlantic Ocean, churning up huge waves and crashing against the rocks along the Irish coastline, before gusting across the rich, green countryside. The fierce wind roared its way through city and village streets. In the small town of Glenkilty it lifted the tiles and slates off the roofs, rattled the window panes and gates, set the dogs to howling and the cats to hissing, and made the babies and children stir, restless and uneasy, in their sleep.

Mia Murphy snuggled up in bed, pulling the quilt about her, too scared to sleep.

'Are you all right, pet?' asked her grandmother, getting up and checking the window-catch one more time before pulling the curtains firmly closed.

''Tis only a storm. It will blow itself out in a few hours and be gone by morning, I promise.' Granny Rose stood listening to the wind and muttered thoughtfully, 'Although storm winds do bring change.'

She turned back to Mia. 'Will I sit with you for a while longer and finish reading the story?'

Mia nodded. She was glad of her Granny Rose's voice as she read from the book of fairytales. It comforted her and distracted from the wailing of the wind.

Tired, Mia tried to concentrate on the words of the story. In the woods behind their house, the huge trees tossed and bowed all night, groaning as the wind caught their heavy branches. She closed her eyes, listening to the wind whistling through the tree tops until she eventually fell asleep. Granny Rose slowly closed the book and crept from the room. She could sense the change in the air already.

Rory Murphy was woken by all the hullabaloo, and peered out his bedroom window in the grey, early morning light. What a storm!

Light shone from the windows of the house next door and he could hear the crunch of gravel in the driveway. He ran into his sister's bedroom at the front of the house and pulled the curtains apart.

'Mia, wake up! Quick!'

Mia opened her eyes and saw her brother standing at the foot of the bed, his brown hair standing on end.

'Look! There's somebody moving in next door,' Rory whispered.

Mia jumped out of bed and joined him at the window.

Months ago, after poor old Mr Hackett had died, a large, square 'For Sale' sign had been put up outside the house. Then, just a few days ago, a red banner was pasted across it with the word: 'Sold.' Then nothing. Until now.

Curious, they peeped from the window, trying to get a glimpse of the comings and goings down below. In the half light, they watched as two small, bulky looking men carried furniture and packing crates from the van, up the driveway and into the house next door. The wind seemed to catch the men and lift them off their feet and deposit them on the doorstep.

'How strange!' thought Mia.

They stared open-mouthed as a procession of rather ramshackle-looking household goods seemed to fly up the driveway by themselves. The removal men seemed to be almost running after them! A lampstand, a small round table, a comfortable-looking chair, a dozen fat, red cushions.

Mia jumped up and down with excitement.

'Crazy!' said Rory.

A black jalopy of a bicycle, with a wicker basket and bell on its front, seemed to pedal itself up the driveway. Now, who could own that? No kid would be seen dead on such an ancient bike. Still, what a marvellous contraption! It was followed by a hatstand, an enormous vase, a bright, multicoloured patchwork quilt, a mop and a sweeping brush, each one in turn caught by the wind, swooping and twirling as it was lifted up and carried towards the house.

'How did they do that?' murmured Mia, crouching up on the window seat.

By now, they were both really curious about who was moving in next door. Rory could almost read his sister's mind – she was hoping for a family of girls. He, of course, wanted it to be a boy his own age, so that they could play football together, or go exploring in the back woods. Judging by the assortment of ancient clutter being carried into The Elms, neither of them was in luck. Rory shrugged his shoulders. Sensing Mia's disappointment, he gave her a clumsy hug.

'You've still got me!'

She barely nodded. He guessed having a twelve-year-old brother wasn't much fun for a eleven-year-old girl.

The removal men stepped back into the van and emerged from its shadows with what seemed like a metal box or cage, covered by a black blanket. An old lady suddenly appeared from nowhere, darting in and out beside them. Caught in the wind, she flew around the men, giving orders, directing them up the driveway. She was small and dainty and clad from top to toe in black, the wind catching her long skirt and wrap-around jacket. Her face was hidden by a wide-brimmed, black hat which was tied firmly to her head like a bonnet. Her tiny legs and feet, though encased in clumpy black boots, fought to stay on the ground as she was tossed about and lifted into the air.

'She looks like she's about to blow away,' murmured Mia.

Rory gazed at her too, and wondered what on earth she had

in that big, black covered box of hers. Whatever it was, the men were handling it very carefully, as if it was precious glass.

The two children watched as the men struggled to manoeuvre the black box, trying not to let it fly away in the wind or get bumped as they trundled up the uneven gravel of the driveway. The old woman jumped in and out between them, shouting at them and checking the load.

Suddenly she stopped. Her head spun around and tilted upwards. Rory and Mia could see her face clearly.

'She's ancient!' gasped Rory, shocked by the strange, withered face and piercing, grey eyes that looked in their direction.

Mia stood transfixed. The old woman was staring right up at the window, right up at *her*. Her gaze was unflinching, as if she had expected to find Mia there, waiting and watching.

Rory pulled at his sister's sleeve, dragging her away from the window. Something in the old woman's gaze had unsettled him, too.

'She's just weird.'

'She's like a witch, Rory!' said Mia, anxiously. 'A witch in a story, in a book. She was staring at me. I could feel her eyes right on me.'

They stood hidden behind the blue-and-white gingham curtains as the old woman seemed to sniff the air, almost like a bloodhound. Then, with what looked like a smile, she turned away and set about the rest of her moving, the wind lifting her on to the doorstep.

By the time bright shafts of early morning sunshine lit the sky, the mysterious wind had softened to a gentle breeze. It was breakfast time in the Murphy household, and time to get ready for school. The brown van had disappeared along the lake road, back towards Glenkilty and their new neighbour had moved in, shutting her hall door firmly.

'She's a witch,' thought Mia to herself, sitting at the table in her school uniform, eating her breakfast, 'and she's come to live next door!'

Chapter 2

The Witch Next Door

'The old woman next door's a bit odd!' sighed the children's mother, Helen Murphy, sitting at the dinner table that evening, a worried frown creasing her forehead. 'I called around today, just to be neighbourly, with an apple tart and some of Granny's home-made jam and a few flowers from the garden, and she wouldn't even open the door. I could see her inside, moving around. But she didn't bother to come to the door. Isn't that strange?'

'What about the apple tart, Mum?' asked Rory, hoping they'd have it for dinner.

'Oh, I left the welcome presents on the front step for her, but it just seems strange to move all the way out here to the country and not want to get to know your neighbours.'

'She's probably a very private kind of person who just wants to keep herself to herself,' suggested Matthew, the children's father.

Rory and Mia glanced at each other.

'So you two keep out of her way, do you hear me!' he added.

They didn't need telling twice. Both of them had already made up their minds that the eccentric old woman was best avoided.

'I don't like her, anyway!' said Mia softly.

'How can you not like someone when you don't even know them? Don't be silly, Mia,' said her mother.

'I just don't!' Mia insisted stubbornly.

Granny Rose handed Mia the big bowl of mashed potato. 'Why, Mia?'

Mia hesitated. She could never hide anything from Granny Rose and was about to say how she knew the old woman was really a witch when Rory winked at her and gave a sudden belch, loud and huge. Mia burst out laughing. Granny covered her mouth trying to disguise her own smiles, while Rory got a long lecture on good manners from his parents.

✧ ◆ ✧

Jackie's barking woke Rory early on Sunday morning. Their small Jack Russell terrier was going crazy, racing up and down the back garden in a frenzy. She was trying to jump up into the trees, hurtling her small body up in the air, and barking wildly at an amazing assortment of birds flying across the garden, that swooped down and skimmed the hedge before landing on next door's lawn.

Magpies, crows, rooks, starlings, plump wood pigeons, sleek blackbirds, brown speckled thrushes and chubby little robins – Rory had never seen the like of it. Almost every piece of grass or earth was covered by some kind of feathered creature, and as Rory looked down from his bedroom window, he saw their new neighbour standing there in the middle of them all.

The old woman wore a loose, blue dressing gown, and her white hair streamed over her shoulders. The birds made soft cooing noises and throaty caws as she stepped daintily amongst them. She talked continuously to them and touched their smooth black, grey and blue heads. Their darting eyes were fixed on her as she spoke. Even the huge, grey heron that lived on the lake stood to attention, listening. Like a group of soldiers taking orders from a commanding officer, they waited patiently until, with a clap of her hands, she dismissed them. Then the flapping of hundreds of wings filled the air as they all lifted into the sky.

Rory watched in amazement as they flew off in different directions, in towards Glenkilty, out across the lake, up to the busy motorway and the city itself beyond, and back into the darkness of the wood. Jackie tried to launch herself after them like a small, white fur bomb, stopping only when the old woman was left standing alone in her garden. Rory sat on his bed wondering at the strange phenomenon he had witnessed. He decided not to mention it to Mia as she already had enough weird notions about their next-door neighbour, and was already frightened of her.

The grass began to grow long and wild in the old woman's garden. Weeds pushed up through the earth and through every crack and crevice in the gravel driveway. The tall, sprawling hedge which formed a barrier between the two houses was left unchecked. The Murphys longed for the familiar sound of Mr Hackett's lawnmower or clipping shears rather than the silence that enveloped the house next door for most of the day.

The flocking of birds early in the morning had become a regular occurrence – the Murphys now referred to their strange neighbour as the Bird Woman.

Mia worried about the Bird Woman all the time, and took the utmost care not to see, or be seen by the old lady.

'Why did *she* have to come and live beside *us*!' she said again and again. 'Why did *she* have to go and choose a house in Glenkilty, next door to *us*?'

Sometimes Mia shut her eyes as she walked by the house so she wouldn't catch a glimpse of the dark figure staring out at her from the upstairs window.

✧ ★ ✧

One Saturday afternoon, Dad had taken over the sitting room and was rehearsing his latest magic trick for the hundredth time – how to make a bunch of silk flowers change into Snowy, their rabbit. Snowy was being difficult and kept popping out ahead of time, showing a twitching nose or fluffy tail where it was not meant to be. Rory and Mia had to sit, squashed alongside Mum and Granny on the couch, pretending to be the audience – and trying not to notice Snowy's bad timing. Rory sighed to himself. Why did his father have to have such a stupid hobby? Why couldn't Matthew Murphy join a golf club or play tennis, or even go jogging around the lanes of Glenkilty like other boys' fathers, instead of being a member of the Celtic Amateur Magicians' Association? It was dead embarrassing.

'If you two are going to keep giggling and putting your Dad off his stride you should go outside and play,' warned Granny, who often boasted proudly of having bought Dad his very first magic set.

Not waiting to be told again, Mia and Rory jumped up, glad to leave the rehearsal. Grabbing the football from the understairs cupboard, they raced outside to the back garden, into the fresh air and sunshine.

'Kick it hard!' Rory yelled at Mia. 'Try and score a goal past me.'

The two of them kicked the ball back and forth to each other. Mia was good at football. Living so far out of town, she usually ended up playing with Rory, and she could play football and rounders and cricket as well as most boys her age. Rory tried to tackle her now as she dribbled the ball past him. Mia gave the ball a mighty kick, sending it flying across the garden, high over his head. He stared, disgusted, as the heavy ball soared over the thick, green hedge and straight into the jungle of grass and weeds next door.

'What did you do that for?' Rory yelled.

'I didn't mean to! It just went high and...'

'You get it!' he shouted at her.

Mia stood shaking her head vehemently, her long, wavy tossing hair from side to side.

'I'm not going into the witch's garden!' she said fiercely. 'You go!'

'*You* kicked it in!'

They argued back and forth, neither of them wanting to go through the narrow gap in the hedge.

But Rory loved that leather ball and wasn't prepared to lose it.

'Come on, then!' he said, 'we'll both go!'

Time had worn a hole in the hedge, leaving a gap which the children had used regularly to visit Mr Hackett. They could still just about squeeze through it. The garden was in a mess and wildly overgrown. They searched through the weeds and nettles and thistles, but there was no sign of their ball. It must have rolled up near the house. Holding their breaths and treading quietly, they began to search nearer and nearer to the house. They could see the drawing room and the kitchen, and the round glasshouse which clung giddily to the back of the house. Mr Hackett had loved cacti and rare plants, and he had practically lived in his glasshouse. Heavy blinds covered the glass today.

There was no sign of the football and they were just about

to give up and leave when they heard a voice.

'The children! The children from next door!'

The old woman stood in front of them. Neither of them had heard her come into the garden. Mia gasped and jumped behind Rory, trying to hide.

Rory held his ground. He stared at the old woman. She looked different today, ordinary almost. Up close, she was just like anyone's granny or favourite old aunt, in her pale blue tweed suit, hushpuppy shoes like their own Granny Rose wore, her white hair pulled back in a soft bun, her face powdered slightly, and a pair of gold-rimmed glasses.

'Welcome, my dears! You're both very welcome. I knew there were children next door, and it's so nice to meet you at last. I must thank your good mother for the gifts she left on my doorstep. It was kind of her.'

Mia smiled shyly. Rory felt uneasy.

The Bird Woman laughed, a soft, tinkling kind of laugh. 'Oh, goodness, I must introduce myself. I'm Mrs Blackwell. Bella Blackwell.'

'And I'm Mia, Mia Murphy. I'm eleven,' volunteered Mia, much to Rory's amazement. She stepped forward. 'And this is Rory, my brother, and he's twelve.'

'We were just looking for our football,' stammered Rory, anxious to get out of the place and wondering what on earth had come over Mia.

'I'm sure we'll find it,' smiled Mrs Blackwell. 'But why don't you come inside first and have some blackcurrant juice and one of my oatmeal cookies?'

Before Rory had a chance to say anything, Mia was already ahead of him, following the woman inside the house. He had no option but to go after them.

They had been in this house many times before, but without Mr Hackett's furniture and old ornaments it looked different and felt strange. Rory sat on the edge of a lumpy, red couch in the sitting room. Mia had gone off into the kitchen to help Mrs Blackwell. Rory wondered why there were no photos of Mr Blackwell, or any family members on top of the bureau or sideboard. Old people usually liked to have photos around them.

Mia was chatting away happily when she reappeared carrying a plate of cookies, the old woman following her with a jug and three glasses.

'I feel I know your family already,' said Mrs Blackwell, looking quizzically at Rory as she poured out a glass of purplish juice for him. 'Mia has told me so much about you all.'

Rory glared at his sister, wishing that she would keep that big mouth of hers shut. Mia smirked and wrinkled her nose to show that she didn't care what he thought, before nibbling her cookie. Rory decided that he wasn't hungry, and he found the drink too sickly sweet for his liking. He sipped unenthusiastically.

'Just imagine, a magician living next door!' the old lady exclaimed. 'Mia told me your father is a magician, Rory. How wonderful!'

Rory stared at the patterned rug on the floor. How could Mia be so stupid!

'Actually, Dad's a bank manager, Mrs Blackwell. He works in town. The magic stuff he does is just a sort of hobby,' he corrected her.

The old woman smiled knowingly. 'A hobby,' she laughed, leaning forward towards him. 'Is that what he calls it?'

'Honestly,' protested Rory, 'it's just party tricks and stuff like that. He's just an amateur.'

'I think Daddy's quite good at magic,' interrupted Mia, 'and he's getting better.'

The old woman and the girl smiled at each other as if they shared a secret, leaving Rory feeling left out and jealous. He remembered the football.

'If you don't mind, Mrs Blackwell,' he said, 'I want to try and find my ball.' He stood up, putting his glass on the wobbly-looking side-table. 'Thank you for the drink. Are you coming, Mia?'

His sister seemed to hesitate for a second, but then sensing his mood followed his example and stood up too.

'Good gracious!' murmured Mrs Blackwell. 'It's been so nice meeting children again, it's been such a long time ... I mean, such nice children...'

'Thank you, Mrs Blackwell,' said Mia. 'I'm sorry we have to go.'

'You'll come again, Mia, now that we are friends,' said the old lady. 'Promise?'

Mia nodded. 'I will.'

Mrs Blackwell led them back outside. Three magpies sitting on the branch of a tree watched them as they stepped back out into the open air.

Rory glanced around the garden, wondering how far the ball could have rolled. He nearly jumped with surprise when he spotted it almost immediately, sitting in front of them on the lawn.

'Oh, there it is, Rory!' said Mia.

I don't believe it, thought Rory. That's weird. There's no way I could have walked past it earlier without seeing it.

'You'll come back soon,' stated Mrs Blackwell, smiling and handing him the ball. But Rory knew that it was Mia she really wanted to see again, not him. Annoyed, he pushed his sister ahead of him through the gap in the hedge.

'Why did you have to go tell her things?' he asked Mia angrily. 'She's a daft old woman and now she thinks we're her friends.'

Mia looked puzzled. 'I like her.'

'What about all the things you said – about her being a witch and how she scared you?' he reminded her.

'Did I?'

'Yes, you did!' he insisted.

'Well, I was wrong. She's just a poor old lady with no family of her own. I think she's lonely. She said I'm a magician's daughter ... that's something special.'

There was no point in arguing with Mia once her mind was

made up. Disgruntled, Rory went inside, leaving his sister standing in the garden, the three magpies who had followed them home perched in the cherry tree above her head.

Chapter 3

Bella's Secrets

Mia stood alone in the hallway of The Elms. The back door had been left unlocked and she'd let herself in. It wasn't really trespassing when you were half-expected anyway, she reasoned. She liked to call in to visit the old lady after school most days now, to make sure she was all right and to have a little chat. Already they had become firm friends.

'Mrs Blackwell! Mrs Blackwell!' she called out.

The Bird Woman didn't answer. Mia looked in the sitting room, then the dining room. Perhaps Bella was upstairs having a nap. She didn't dare climb the curving staircase and disturb her.

'Mrs Blackwell!' she called again.

Where could her friend be? The old black bicycle was missing from its spot near the back door. Maybe Bella had gone into the village for something. Mia sighed. It seemed unfair that Bella was not there to meet her, just when she'd managed to finish her homework quickly, avoided unpacking the dishwasher *and* given Rory the slip. It seemed really strange to her now the way her brother had taken such a dislike to Bella. He did everything he could to keep herself and Bella Blackwell apart. Mia may have changed her mind about the old lady, but Rory certainly hadn't.

Mia sat at the kitchen table hoping that Bella would be back any minute. The kitchen was very different from the Murphys' – it was very old fashioned, with a big Aga stove. The windows were small and narrow, and there was an old white sink for doing the washing up, and a couple of shelves and presses, crowded with odds and ends. Mia continued to wait.

The house was silent and still. Then she heard it – a rustling, chirping noise. What was it? Bella must be in the glasshouse!

Mia pulled back the heavy, wine-coloured, velvet curtains of the dining room to reveal the glasshouse entrance. Was this where Mrs Blackwell kept her rare birds?

The door was unlocked, but the heavy, rusted hinges squeaked loudly as she pushed it open. Bleached wooden floorboards stretched the length of the curved building. One glass wall was obscured by a tall array of creepers and huge green plants, another by a long blind.

'Mrs Blackwell,' Mia whispered softly, and stepped inside. 'Are you there?'

A rustling movement was the only answer to her question. Mia pulled the door closed behind her, not wanting any of the birds to escape. There was no sign of Bella.

The glasshouse was warm, humid. Her eyes searched for a glimpse of bright feathers among the green plants. Something brushed against her cheek. Startled, Mia realised it was only a great feathery fern. Then, with a quick flutter something darted toward the glass roof, its reflection catching her eye. She spun around, trying to see what it was.

Another rustling noise sounded overhead. The birds must be hiding in the big old vine that Mr Hackett had planted. Mia craned her neck upwards, trying to get a glimpse of them.

A sudden ripple of wings and fluttering filled the air all around her. Mia jumped backwards and turned to run out of the room. But something flew past her, almost becoming entangled in her hair. Something else swept past her shoulder, while yet another object, light and feathery, brushed against her legs. Terrified, Mia stood perfectly still as a mass of black shapes milled around her. They must be bats! She *hated* bats! She closed her eyes and covered her head with her arms.

The flapping and rustling continued as the small creatures bashed into her. They became more and more frantic. She kept her eyes shut tight, hoping they would stop and leave her alone. Petrified, she stood as still as a garden statue, wishing that the crazy movements would stop so that she could escape.

'Child! Oh, Mia child, don't be scared! They won't hurt or harm you, I promise.'

Mia almost fainted with relief when she heard the old

woman's voice. Forgetting that Bella might be angry with her, she flung herself into the old woman's arms.

'There, there, child!' said Bella, wrapping her arms protectively around the girl. 'Don't take on so! They're almost as scared as you are. Hush, now! Look!'

Mia was too scared to open her eyes, but finally, at Bella's insistence, she took a cautious look.

At first she could see nothing. The deep green of the fluttering vine leaves hid a dark shape that lay camouflaged within them. She could barely make out the outline. It was some kind of a flying lizard. Two bright eyes stared at her. Then the creature moved closer, its large snout and nostrils quivering. Mia could see the high curve of its leathery wings and noticed its fine, curving tail. Gasping with amazement she realised that this was no ordinary lizard. In fact, it looked like a dragon! Smaller than any she'd ever read about or seen pictures of, nonetheless ... it *was* a dragon.

The small, black dragon stared back at her. Suddenly there were dragons all about her, shiny-eyed, inquisitive, watching, chirping in high-pitched tones. Mia blinked, afraid. She was imagining it, she must be. There was no such thing as dragons! They existed only in fairytales.

'My dragons!' said Bella proudly, staring at Mia. 'Now you have discovered my secret.'

'Are they really dragons?'

'Yes, of course, child. But don't be afraid, they're still dragonlings yet. They won't harm you.'

Putting her teeth together, and making a gentle, clicking sound, Bella called to a dragon that was hidden in the lush greenery.

A young, dusty, gold-coloured creature wriggled forward, his tail wagging wildly as Bella began to pat his long neck and talk to him.

'That's a good boy, Oro, good boy.'

Mia could see that the dragon loved the attention, just like a dog or cat.

'Touch him!' ordered Bella softly.

Mia drew back. She didn't want to touch these weird lizard things that the old woman thought were dragons. This one's skin looked scaly like a snake's, but yet dry and leathery. His green eyes narrowed and he stared at her as if he might attack or bite her.

'Go on!'

She barely touched the creature with her finger, but was surprised by his warmth. Braver now, she traced her finger gently along his side. He turned his neck and head around to sniff her. Satisfied, he let her pet him.

'There!' said Bella, her eyes shining.

Still nervous, Mia tried to ignore the rustling and fluttering as the rest of the dragons pushed forward, jostling for attention.

'They like you,' laughed the old woman.

All about the glasshouse, hidden in the trailing plants and tall, deep green vines, lizards or dragons or whatever they were, were watching her, their eyes glinting. Mia had never seen or imagined anything like them.

'You did well, magician's daughter. Conquering fear of the old or new is no easy thing. The dragonlings will sense that and be your friends. Already you know by instinct how to calm and soothe them.'

Mia felt bewildered. She didn't know what to make of the strange old lady and her dragons. Could it possibly be real?

'Come, Mia, you and I must talk,' said Bella, suddenly dismissing Oro. Mia followed nervously behind her as she closed the glasshouse door and stepped back into the dining room.

They walked down into the kitchen, where the old woman sat down on a rocking chair and pulled out a stool for Mia.

'Are you all right, child?'

Mia nodded. Her heart was beating like a drum and she wondered if she should run away home – but something made her want to stay and listen to Bella.

'Are they really dragons? Really?'

Yes, child, yes!' answered Bella excitedly. 'Haven't you seen them with your own eyes, touched one? These dragons are real enough, all right.'

'I thought dragons were just make-believe, something you read about in fairy stories,' murmured Mia. 'I still can't believe it. Dragons really exist!'

Bella laughed. 'There have always been dragons, Mia. Humans have always feared them and fought them and tried to capture them. How do you think dragons found their way into so many stories and legends, only that people saw them

and believed in them? Dragon lore passed from one genera-
tion to another, some written down, some just remembered.'

'But how did the dragons get *here*? Here in Glenkilty?
Where did you find them?'

'In the wood.' Bella pointed towards the window.

'Glenkilty Wood!' gasped Mia. '*Our* wood!'

'Aye. It was terrible. Men came with their great yellow
monsters of machines and attacked the wood. They tore
down the trees, uprooted them, turning over the sacred soil.
They broke the bones of old ones as they used giant, buzzing
saw weapons to cut the trees down. I witnessed it with my
own eyes. The dragons were no longer safe, the woods could
no longer protect them from humans.'

'They're building the Glenkilty by-pass road, cutting
through the edge of the wood,' explained Mia.

'It was Providence that I found these hatchlings, hidden
for so long in a circle of stones. I saved them from the jaws of
those great iron machines. They need protecting and minding, especially in this world of yours, until they are strong and
fit enough to return with me to a world where they will be safe
and free. I've been minding dragons ever since I was a young
girl, Mia. Big ones, little ones, brave ones and, though it pains
me to admit it, some pure evil ones. My job has always been to
look after the dragons.'

'I don't understand,' mumbled Mia, not managing to make
any sense of what Bella was saying.

'These dragonlings are perhaps the only dragons left in the

world. They have survived for many years, centuries even. Do you realise how precious and rare they are, how important? Hunger and disease and the ravages of war and greed destroyed the rest of the dragons. They were hunted down until their species was almost entirely extinct.

'Long, long ago, the Great Mage ordered that dragonkind would remain hidden for a thousand years, until the coming of the next millennium and the new age of peace and magic. A new dawn. A new beginning. But humankind has forgotten all that was promised.' The old woman shook her head sorrowfully. 'I'm not sure if humankind will ever learn to live without the evils of war, but I have been entrusted with the care of these young dragons to ensure their survival.'

Mia tried to understand what the old woman was talking about as she rambled on about magicians, yellow monsters and dragons. She was still scared and longed to be back in her own home sitting in front of the fire with the television on.

Bella's thin, bony hands reached out to her.

'Time is running out, child. I'm old, too old. My time has nearly come. You are young, a magician's daughter, no less. 'Tis destiny that led me here to the edge of this wood to find the dragons and to find you. Nothing happens by accident. A mage can always sense the presence of another close by. That is why I chose you, Mia. You must help. You will be my apprentice. You will help me with the dragons and learn the old ways, while there is still time for me to pass on the wisdom before I die!'

Mia was really frightened now. For the first time she noticed how the wrinkles on Bella's face resembled a map, and the veins on her brow were shaped like a dragon's wings.

'I have to go home!' Mia blurted out. 'My Mum will be mad at me if I'm late for dinner, honest. She doesn't even know I'm here.'

Bella Blackwell gave a slow nod. 'You will return!' she said emphatically, and grasped Mia's arm.

Mia jumped up off the stool and forced the gnarled fingers apart.

'Let me go!' she screamed, and she raced out the door, running away from the old woman and her mad talk.

'Don't go, child!' pleaded the dragon woman. 'Don't go!'

Mia turned to go down the driveway. She watched in disbelief as, ahead of her, the heavy, iron gates began to shut, blocking her escape. Terrified, she raced around the side of the house to the back garden.

She hurled herself through the gap in the hedge, dry branches scraping her skin, grass and mud sticking to her clothes. She almost cried with relief when Jackie's wet nose greeted her at the other side. Grabbing the small dog up in her arms, she ran in to the house, locking the door behind her.

Chapter 4

Glenkilty Wood

Mia was always fearful now. At night, her dreams were filled with dragons and monsters and a constant whispering voice that pleaded with her to return to return to the house next door. Had Bella put a spell on her? Enchanted her? She tried to convince herself that what she had seen in the glass-house had been an illusion, a trick, a hologram even. But she only had to look out of the back window of her house and see the familiar curved structure of the glasshouse, to remember vividly the flutter of dragon wings, the glimmer of dragon eyes and the feel of dragon skin.

The following week, Bella cycled down by the lake and along the village road every day, passing by Glenkilty National School. Dressed heavily in black, she rode her old black bicycle in front of the school yard. Mia watched from the classroom window, anxious and afraid, hearing Bella call her name again and again. Neither the teacher nor the other children seemed to notice anything.

When Mia was going to the supermarket, or the post office or just even walking home from school, she knew that Bella would suddenly appear, smiling and friendly. She did her best to stay close to her Mum and her Granny and her friends, but she knew that they could not protect her forever from Bella's magic.

'Are you all right, pet?' asked Mum, sensing that something was going on.

'Yep!' said Mia, too frightened to tell. She didn't want to be an apprentice dragon keeper, or helper or whatever that crazy old witch wanted of her. She just wanted to go back to being a normal eleven-year-old girl who knew nothing about dragons or magic or people's time running out!

The whole family had noticed Mia's behaviour and they were beginning to get very worried.

'There's definitely something wrong with Mia,' Granny Rose said as she rolled out pastry for an apple tart on the kitchen table.

'Rory, do you think Mia's being bullied at school or something like that?' asked Mum, a worried frown creasing her forehead.

He didn't think so. Mia would tell him something like that, he was sure.

But Mum and Granny were right. Something was wrong with his sister. She seemed tense and nervous, as if she was scared of something or had a big secret to keep.

'It's that Bella Blackwell, next door. She has something to do with it, I'll be bound,' Granny said, shaking her head.

'The two of you have always been so close, Rory. Will you have a word with her?' begged Mum.

'I'll try and talk to her,' he promised.

✧ ★ ✧

Jackie raced in front of them snuffling at the leaves, as Rory and Mia walked through Glenkilty Wood. Rory was glad that he's managed to persuade his sister to put on her new yellow padded jacket and join him, for the woods behind their house had always been a favourite place of theirs. Oak, ash and chestnut trees formed a natural tunnel of greenery, and as they walked, the sunlight flickered and danced through the leaves. Only Jackie's panting and the crackle of broken twigs disturbed the silence. Druids, hermits, bandits and outlaws were all supposed to have found shelter within Glenkilty's ancient wood many centuries ago.

'I want to see down by the roadworks,' said Mia, startling Rory from his daydream.

At the edge of the wood they both stopped, horrified by the decimated area where huge trees had been removed to make room for road widening. Cars and trucks would soon replace green leaves and tree trunks.

'It has been destroyed,' said Rory, sadly.

Mia searched among the enormous tree trunks cut close to the ground. Bending down low she scrabbled among the scattered sawdust and timber until she found what she wanted. There it was, a large circle of rounded stones placed near to each other, almost covered by bracken and ferns.

'That's funny,' said Rory, 'I never noticed them before.'

✧ ◆ ✧

Rory had put two chocolate bars in his pocket. Fresh air and exercise always made him hungry. Deep in the woods there was a clearing where wooden picnic tables had been set up for the summer visitors. Rory sat down on one of the benches and passed Mia some chocolate.

She nibbled it slowly, like a small rabbit, leaving teeth marks in the bar. A fat wood pigeon strutted by, pecking at the ground.

'I bet she sent him to spy on me,' Mia muttered to herself, shooing the bird away.

'Is everything all right, Mia?' Rory asked softly.

He could see a flicker of indecision cross her face.

'I don't know what to do, Rory, I'm scared and ...' His sister looked around as if checking her surroundings. 'Do you believe in magic, Rory?'

Surprised by her question, he began to laugh, ignoring her dismay.

'You mean like Dad!' he jeered. 'No way! It's just tricks

and sleight of hand and practice, that's all magic is.'

'No, I mean proper magic,' she insisted.

'Hocus pocus! I don't believe any of that kind of stuff,' he said firmly. 'You know that! There's always a logical reason for things. An explanation.'

Mia smiled nervously. 'What about Bella? You saw her too, Rory. Bella can do magic! You know she can!'

'The Bird Woman! Is that what's upset you?'

'She's not a Bird Woman!' Mia shouted angrily at him. 'She's a Dragon Woman, a Dragon Keeper!'

'A Dragon Woman!' he burst out laughing. 'I don't believe it, Mia! Where on earth did you get such a crazy idea from? Dragons! They don't exist! They're just a myth, part of old legends!'

'They do exist!' she screamed at him. 'I've *seen* them!'

'You thought you saw them, imagined you saw them!' he insisted. Perhaps that old witch or whatever she is conjured them up, or hypnotised you. Be sensible, Mia, there's no such thing as dragons, not really!'

'You play with dragons, I've seen you, Rory.'

'That's on the computer. They're just games. Made-up, animated, computer-generated images of dragons and monsters, whatever. They're not real, it's just for fun!'

'But someone must have seen them once. How else would they know how to draw them?'

'They imagined them,' he retorted firmly.

'The other day I was looking for Bella, Rory, and I went

into the glasshouse. Remember when Mr Hackett had it and it was full of all his plants? Do you know what Bella has hidden there? Dragons, small baby dragons. Dragonlings. I saw them. I swear! She found them in that circle of stones at the edge of the woods. She says that they're the last surviving dragons in the world. They're so small they look almost like big lizards. Bella says that she wants me to help her, to become her apprentice. She says she's too old, that she wants to teach me all she knows about them and show me what to do before her time runs out!' Mia, pale and breathless, let the words come tumbling out, fast and furious, her voice shaking.

'They're dragons, baby dragons, I saw them, Rory, honest I did! I touched one, felt his skin, and ran my fingers along his backbone. I saw his eyes. It was a real dragon, Rory, I'm not imagining it, honest I'm not!'

Rory didn't know what to think. How could Mia actually believe that their crazy neighbour had found dragons here in Glenkilty Wood? It was bad enough that the old woman was obviously bonkers, but now she was putting her strange ideas into Mia's head too.

'It's not true, Mia! I don't care what that old woman told you, or what you think you saw, none of it is true. Don't believe it, any of it!' he shouted angrily at her.

'The thing is ...' said Mia softly, 'I do!'

In the distance, Jackie suddenly whined, then barked.

'She must be stuck. I'll go get her!' Rory said.

Mia stayed sitting on the log, a small, scared figure.

Jackie was caught in a small patch of briars, which she had run into in her haste to catch something or other, probably a squirrel or a rabbit. Untangling the squirming dog took Rory a few minutes, and by the time he walked the few yards back, Mia was gone. He saw the yellow flash of her jacket way ahead of him on the path. He called and called her, but she ignored him and kept walking on.

Mia didn't know what to do. Talking to Rory hadn't helped at all. Usually her brother was so understanding. They'd always helped each other and stood up for each other no matter what, but now they seemed so far apart. He didn't believe her and she wasn't prepared to listen to him.

She had never felt so alone and unsure of herself. All her life she had been reading books and listening to stories, stories about princes and princesses and giants and dwarves, witches and wizards and all kinds of incredible happenings – children who followed a piper and were never seen again, a king who turned everything he touched into gold, a mermaid who sold her beautiful voice for a pair of human legs, why, even her mother and grandmother had told her about the banshee that cried the night before anyone in their family died, and of the little man who, if you managed to catch him, would share his crock of gold with you at the end of the rainbow. Her head and heart were full of such stories, they filled her brain and she dreamed and imagined them in the long hours of night. Were they all nothing but lies, based on nothing more real than imagination? Surely strange things could and did happen in the world?

She was tired of being scared and worrying about Bella. The dragons meant her no harm. She had not just imagined them, or made them up! They *were* real.

Walking back home she felt more light-hearted, clear-headed. She stopped outside the witch's house, staring up at the windows, almost unafraid. She was just turning up the driveway to her own house when Dad pulled up in the car. He stopped and parked and reached into the back seat for his briefcase.

'Everything okay, Mia?' he asked, hugging her. 'Were you in next door?'

She looked at him, standing there beside her. He was tall and sandy-haired, balding in the front, wearing a navy suit, a white shirt and a multicoloured, striped tie. He always seemed out of step with the world and what was going on around him, as if he lived in a world of his own that was more real to him than the actual world. It drove her mother mad and exasperated Rory.

'Bella, the old woman next door keeps dragons, Dad,' she blurted out. 'There are eight of them!'

Matthew Murphy looked across at The Elms, his eyes studying the shape and form of the old house before coming to rest on the windows.

'Does she indeed! What colour are they?'

Mia stood in disbelief. Her father hadn't shouted or roared

at her, or even argued about the existence of dragons.

'There are two black ones and a gold one, and four green ones and a blue one.'

'How interesting!' nodded her father.

'Oh Daddy, I love you!' Mia smiled and gave him a big hug.

Matthew Murphy was left standing there, wondering what it was he had said or done that pleased his daughter so much.

Chapter 5

The Apprentice

'So you came back, child. You returned to see Bella and the dragons.' The old woman smiled as she opened the front door to Mia.

Mia stepped across the threshold, realising that she was taking far more than just one simple step by coming back to visit The Elms. By doing so, she was accepting all the old dragon keeper had told her and showing a willingness to listen and learn.

The hall was chilly and she shivered, hoping that she had made the right choice.

'I came to help you,' she said simply.

'Welcome, Mia!' said the old woman, holding her close. 'Come, child, there is much to be done. I was just bringing fresh water and bedding for them. You can give me a hand.'

Mia carried two enormous jugs of water into the glass-house, filled the stone bowls placed on the ground and then helped Bella to carry in bales of straw from the back garden.

A swell of chattering and high-pitched calling greeted her as she brushed the fouled straw into a heap in the corner, then shovelled it into black bin bags. Yuck! Dragons could be very smelly creatures. Opening a fresh bale, she spread the clean straw out on the ground, watching as the animals tossed about in it and moved it into hidden corners.

'Nothing like a nice fresh bed,' she said aloud, wondering if the dragons could understand her. Two of them jumped down, landing close beside her, sniffing curiously.

'They have a very well-developed sense of smell,' stated Bella. 'They're trying to remember your scent. That is one of the ways a dragon can tell the difference between a friend and an enemy.'

Mia hoped that the creatures considered her a friend, because looking at their sharp claws and pointed teeth and their lashing tails, she certainly would not like to be an enemy.

As they worked, Bella pointed out each dragon, calling them by name and telling her about them.

'Arznel, he's the strongest and the bravest, mark my words. That's a female, Rana, she's as loyal and good-hearted as they come. A willing dragon is always easy to teach.'

Mia spent the whole afternoon working, while at the same time trying to listen and take in all the old woman was telling her. When the late afternoon sun flooded into the glasshouse, it became almost unbearably warm. Raising her arm to wipe the sweat off her forehead, Mia knocked against an enormous potted plant which she tried in vain to steady. From far above came a screaming, whirring sound, as one of the dragons fell with a thud onto the ground in front of her, giving a mew of pain.

'Oh, I'm sorry!' she said, rushing forward.

The dragon seemed smaller than all the others, his muscles less developed. His skin was bluish-green. He lay cowering fearfully and trembling with shock. Mia bent to help him.

'What have you done, Trig?' sighed Bella, exasperated. 'Don't tell me you've fallen again!'

The small, almost-blue dragon seemed to hang his head in shame at the old woman's words.

'He's hurt,' said Mia, defending the poor creature. 'It was all my fault!'

Bella came over beside her, crouching down to inspect the damage, tut-tutting and shaking her head.

'It could be a wing. I need to examine him properly, and he seems to have to damaged a tailbone too. Here, help me move him into the kitchen where I can get a better look at him!'

Mia bent down, unsure of how to lift an injured dragon, and wondering if Trig would bite. The dragon looked up at her steadily, making no objection as she pulled him ever so gently towards her, trying not to touch the small cut she could see on his side.

'That's it,' said Bella, leading her out to the kitchen while at the same time patting the dragon's head. 'There, there, Trig, Mia and I will heal you.'

The old woman spread a thick towel on the kitchen table and gestured to Mia to ease Trig down gently onto it.

Mia watched as Bella ran her hands all over the blue-green skin of the dragon, stretching his good wing wide open as the creature lay still, mewing weakly every now and then. Then she touched the injured wing, showing Mia the spot where his skin lay open, a mottled purple-red bruise staining the skin around it.

'Hold him still, child, while I see what's what. A dragon with an injured wing is not much use for anything.'

As if understanding her, tears welled up in the dragon's green eyes.

'Let me see if I can close this wound and ease the damage.'

The old woman produced two phials of foul-smelling liquid. The first, which was a nasty, dirty brown colour, seemed to be almost like glue and it stuck the edges of the wound together; the other she spread over the general bruising. Then she stroked his tail with her fingers, running them along the bone.

'It's a simple break and should heal of its own accord. Good dragon, Trig, good dragon! Now you must get some rest!'

Mia watched as Bella sat down in her old rocking chair.

'Pass me the dragon, Mia. I will mind him for tonight as he's not well enough to rejoin the rest of them.'

The dragon seemed drowsy and did not object as Mia lowered him onto the old woman's lap.

'There, Mia, child! We'll be fine, now. You run along home

or that old grandmother of yours will be giving out about me again!'

Mia was reluctant to go. She watched as the old woman closed her eyes and drifted off to sleep, the chair gently rocking Bella and the dragon backwards and forwards in a slow, gentle rhythm.

Chapter 6

Trig

Mia went through the gap in the hedge almost every day, checking on the progress of the injured dragon. She still blamed herself for Trig's accident.

'He's not like the others,' said Bella. 'He's not as big or quick or bright. I suppose he's the weakling of the bunch. There always seems to be one, no matter how hard you try to care for them and teach them.'

The old woman herself looked tired. Her face at times had a greyish pallor, and the veins across her brow became a livid purple colour. She looked old and frail, and Mia did her best to help as much as she could, running to the village for groceries, cleaning up the house and caring for the young dragons. She wondered why Bella didn't just use her powers to conjure up some helpers and make things a lot easier for herself.

'I am old, child, and will not waste my magic powers on silly tricks and showing off,' said Bella, reading her mind.

The best thing about going next door was having time to be with the dragons, especially Trig. He was her favourite now. The small, blue-green dragon moved around slowly and stiffly, obviously still in pain, and would look up from where he was sitting, hoping that she would stop to pat him and talk to him, cocking his head to one side, listening to her.

'He won't eat a thing!' complained Bella. 'He's gone right off his food.'

Mia didn't blame him – the pinkish raw meat that Bella cut into thin strips and served to the dragons looked and smelled absolutely disgusting. She didn't dare ask Bella what kind of meat it was.

'Blues are always finicky eaters. Give me greens or blacks any day. I don't know what's to become of him, he's not getting any stronger. A sick dragon is a sorrowful thing to behold, Mia, that is why I worry about this one so much.'

Trig did look miserable. He was certainly not as big or strong or clever as the other dragons, but Mia knew he was bright enough to follow Bella's every move, and to notice everything she herself did when she called to the house.

'He needs so much attention and care,' sighed the old woman,' and I'm old and tired. It's just too much when all the others need looking after too. It's not fair on them.'

Mia didn't know what to say.

'Blues were always difficult to raise, I suppose that's why they were considered precious and rare if they survived.'

'He will survive, Mrs Blackwell. Trig will survive! Won't he?'

Bella turned her head away, refusing to answer. Mia was upset and wondered if the small, blue dragon had understood everything they'd said. Judging by the reproachful look in his shimmering, emerald-coloured eyes, she guessed he had.

'That wing of his is stiff, Mia. I'm not sure if he'll ever be able to fly properly and gain the height a dragon needs, and his tail, I suspect, will always be slightly misshapen, which may cause balance problems. There is nothing more I can do. You know I have to make preparations for my return to Blackwell Castle and my dragon school.'

'What would happen to a dragon that is weak and sick, and cannot fend for itself?' asked Mia.

'Sometimes dragons attack their own kind and kill those they consider weak or sick, though often they will just let them be and watch as nature takes its course,' said the old woman matter-of-factly.

Mia couldn't bear to think of such a thing happening to Trig and was determined to make him better. The small dragon lapped up all the extra attention as Mia spent more and more time with him. She coaxed him from his straw bed in the corner to get up and move around and become more agile. Bella watched approvingly, well pleased with her young apprentice.

Mia also tried to tempt Trig with a variety of foods, saving stuff from her school lunchbox and sneaking things from the fridge at home. Trig would sniff at everything curiously before looking up at her sad-eyed, rejecting the foods he did not like. By accident she discovered he loved apples and made sure to bring some every day. He also liked cheese and crackers and carrots and grapes. He adored chocolate, but she was sure it was bad for him and pretended not to have any more.

'You'd best get home,' suggested Bella, one dismal grey evening. ''Tis beginning to rain.'

Mia patted each of the dragons goodbye, before putting up her pink umbrella and letting herself out the back door. It was lashing rain, the water bouncing off the umbrella as she tried to run through the wet grass. Her trouser ends and shoes got soaked. Her heart sank knowing the trouble she'd be in for staying out on such an evening. Trying to think of some excuse, Mia became aware of a whining cry close by. Was it Jackie? Something moved behind her, she could sense it.

'Trig!' she cried.

She almost jumped out of her skin, seeing the young dragon following her.

'What are you doing, you silly thing!' she said, running back to him. He was soaking wet but oblivious to this, he butted her playfully with his snout.

'You should be inside!' she scolded, trying to sound cross with him. 'You'll catch cold! What will Bella say about this?'

As if understanding, the dragon dropped his head, whimpering quietly.

'You can't come home with me,' she explained firmly. 'I wish you could Trig, but you just can't.'

Putting down her umbrella, she managed to half turn and lift the dragon. The two of them getting soaked through, rain dripping down her face and eyes, as stumbling she awkwardly carried Trig back to the house.

The old woman opened the door before she even had a chance to knock.

'So, he followed you.'

Panting and out of breath, Mia was glad to put the heavy young dragon down on the kitchen table and hand him over to Bella.

'He must have escaped somehow, he was behind me, luck-ily I heard him and I–'

'Trig has chosen you to be his keeper, Mia. Dragons do that. It is a bond that is not easily broken,' said the old woman seriously.

Mia did not know what to say, but she could see a new respect in Bella's eyes. Soaked to the skin, her long, wet hair plastered to her scalp, she sighed.

'I have to go home,' she explained. 'I'm in enough trouble already, but tell Trig I'll see him again tomorrow – I promise!'

Chapter 7

Granny Rose

The Murphys couldn't understand it. Mia was spending every spare minute of her time with the old Bird Woman. What the two of them talked about or did was a total mystery to everyone else. Mia raced through her homework every evening, and no longer bothered with her favourite television programmes in her rush to visit Bella.

'I asked Mia if she would she like to have some friends over after school,' said her mother, perplexed, 'and she tells me she's too busy. None of her friends have been here for weeks! You know, I met Mrs Blackwell the other day when I was shopping and she seems a nice, gentle sort of person, slightly eccentric, perhaps, but for the life of me I cannot understand why Mia is so taken with her.'

Since the day in the woods, Rory knew that Mia had been avoiding him. He wondered sometimes whether the conversation about imaginary dragons had actually taken place. Mia had made no further mention of any such creatures since. He missed playing and hanging around with her, but he was busy finishing a project for school on the Romans – he had to make a model of the Coliseum out of cardboard. As well as that, he was playing in the football league finals after school. Anyway, his sister seemed happy enough without him, so why should he worry.

Mum and Dad were preparing for a trip to America where Dad was to take part in the annual Amateur Magicians of the World Convention in Las Vegas.

'You will keep an eye on Mia while we're away, Rory? I can rely on you to look after your sister, can't I?' Mum said, looking somewhat worried.

'Of course, Mum,' he promised. 'Granny and Mia and I will be fine. Don't worry about us!'

✧ ✦ ✧

The day of their departure finally came. Mum was busy checking passports and airline tickets and American dollars, and singing 'Viva, Las Vegas' under her breath when she thought no one was listening

Rory helped Dad carry the suitcases and his props out to the car. He had never seen his Dad look so happy and excited. For the past two days he had rehearsed non-stop, perfecting his routine. His new trick, The Chinese Dragon, was amazing. A cardboard dragon would suddenly appear from a cloud of smoke and belch smoke and flames at the audience.

'Have you got everything, Matt?' asked Mum, checking the boot and the back seat.

His father did a quick mental check. Everything seemed to be in order. He reminded Rory of a great explorer setting out on an adventure.

'We'd better hurry,' said Dad, 'or we'll miss our flight.'

Mum gave them all a last hug and goodbye kiss.

'Are you sure you'll be able to manage, Rose, that the children won't be too much for you?'

Granny pretended to look offended. 'It's only for a few weeks, Helen. We'll be just fine. You and Matt go and enjoy yourselves in America. We'll be dying to hear all about it.'

Rory and Mia and their grandmother stood watching as Mum and Dad drove off towards Glenkilty. They were flying to San Francisco first, and then on to Las Vegas. Mia was in a bit of a huff, she hated it when Mum and Dad went away and left her, even if Granny was in charge.

That evening, Mia was even more annoyed. She'd helped tidy up after tea and swept the kitchen floor, and yet Granny was insisting she stay home.

'What are you going around to Mrs Blackwell's for, Mia? What do you do next door, pet?'

Mia just shrugged her shoulders.

'Mrs Blackwell is very old,' began Rose Murphy. 'She's even older than I am. I know what a good, kind, sweet-hearted girl you are, Mia, but nobody expects you to spend every minute of your time with her.'

'But I like going next door,' Mia protested. 'Nobody minded when Rory used go to see Mr Hackett all the time when he lived there.'

'That was different,' interrupted Rory. 'He used to help me build my airfix planes, and taught me how to play chess.'

'Well, Mrs Blackwell teaches me things too.'

'What sort of things, Mia?' quizzed her grandmother.

'All about the olden days.'

'Olden days?'

'Long ago, centuries ago, before you were born, Granny.'

'Ah, history! What else do you do?'

'I just help her, that's all.'

'That glasshouse of hers is magnificent. Do you help her out there?' asked Granny, staring at her.

Mia blushed.

'Is she growing plants in it like Barney Hackett did?'

Mia looked uncomfortable, unsure of what to say.

'Is it like an aviary? Filled with birds?' asked Rory. 'Is that it? Mrs Blackwell loves birds, doesn't she?'

Grateful to her brother, Mia just nodded. She didn't want to deceive her family and tell lies, but she had to protect Bella and the dragons.

'Was that a bird I saw you with the other night – you were carrying it in next door?' asked Granny.

Glad of her Granny's poor eyesight, Mia tried to think of what to say without telling a blatant lie.

'It strayed outside, Granny. The poor thing got injured a while ago and I managed to catch it for Bella.'

'You're a good girl, Mia. I'm lucky to have such a grand-daughter.'

Suddenly, as if realising that she had said too much, Mia stood up to go.

'Listen, Mia, pet, I'd prefer if you didn't go next door this evening. If you want to do something useful, why don't you put the lead on poor Jackie and take her for a walk.' Granny Rose watched the expression on Mia's face carefully.

Mia didn't know what to say. Why was Granny being such an interfering old busybody? Grabbing the dog's lead, she ran out the back door, Jackie yelping with delight and in a frenzy of excitement at the prospect of a walk.

Rose Murphy sighed as her granddaughter left the room. 'Rory, things are much worse than I expected. Mia is obsessed with that woman. She's in great danger and we must try to protect her.'

Rory was stunned. This was a bit over the top. He came over and sat down near Granny. He was really fond of her and always did as she told him to, but what she was saying sounded barmy. He looked at her closely. Rose Murphy was a big, broad, strong, sensible Wicklow woman, not given to superstitious talk, and he knew she would move heaven and earth for the sake of her family.

'Mia's all right, Granny. Don't worry about her.'

'I can't help it, Rory. You know, you and Mia are so different! You're so practical, but your sister lives in her imagination. She's caught up in something now, I can sense it.'

'You think the Bird Woman is dangerous?'

'Aye,' murmured Granny. 'What would the likes of that Bella Blackwell want with your sister? Has she no family or grandchildren of her own? I can't figure it out. It's as if she's put a spell on the child, bewitched her. Why would the old woman do such a thing?'

Rory could see Granny was getting agitated. Her face was flushed, her hands were shaking. The situation with Mia and Bella was obviously upsetting her and that worried him.

'I'll look after Mia, Granny, I promise!'

'You're a good boy, Rory. I think I'm beginning to understand the danger Mia faces. Your sister needs to be kept safe, protected.'

'I'll keep a good eye on her, don't you worry,' said Rory, giving his grandmother a hug.

Reassured, Granny Rose took up the newspaper crossword and a pen.

'Conjuring tricks, five letters?'

'Magic,' replied Rory automatically. The two of them finished off the crossword together.

Chapter 8

Dragon Days

The young dragons were getting bigger and stronger everyday. Even Mia realised that they could no longer remain hidden in the glasshouse, for they were rapidly outgrowing the space it provided. They were constantly hungry too, and calling for more and more food.

'They need to learn to hunt and provide some of their own nourishment,' said Bella. 'It's not good for them to be cooped up like this. I caught Arznel and Oro fighting this morning, jostling for territory.'

Worried, Mia reached down and stroked Trig's bumpy forehead. The young dragon still came to her the minute he saw her, snuffling against her, touching her gently with his head, looking for attention. In her mind he was the finest of them all. He might not be as big as the others yet, but to her he seemed more beautiful, better proportioned. The colour of his skin shimmered and changed in the sunlight from a dark, almost blackish blue to the palest soft blue, the colour of a misty sky. The others chattered and chirruped and gave baby dragon roars every now and then, but Trig listened, taking in all that was said to him. His wing was healing, though it was still too soon for him to fly.

'Soon we must leave, child. The dragons cannot stay here any longer. They need space to grow and fly and hunt. It's dangerous for them here now. In Dragon Wood they will be safe. Dragons have lived there for many centuries. Tall trees and silver lakes and vast, grassy plains – there's no finer place for them to grow into the fabulous creatures nature intended. Your world here is no place for them!'

Mia brought her face close to Trig's and stared into his eyes. How could she bear never to see this young dragon again, or listen to Bella's tales of magic and sorcery?

She knew that in the dark of night, Bella had already started to take the dragons out one at a time, letting them fly to test their growing wings. Several times in the past week, hearing the heavy, rapid movement of wings, she'd peeped out her bedroom window to see a nervous dragon lost in the inky sky, an awkward, black shape that seemed like some enormous bird struggling to keep itself up in the air.

'Come with us, Mia!' pleaded the old woman. 'The work with the dragons has only begun. You are young and able and in time will be a powerful dragon keeper – and an even more powerful mage, knowing all the secrets of the old magic. I promise to teach you everything I know, pass on all the wisdom of my many years, and help you to learn the craft of sorcery. Come with me! Be my apprentice and learn all the magic and dragon ways that I can teach you. I am old, and these dragons will need someone to comfort and care for them when I am gone. They already know and love you, magician's daughter. Come with me and fulfil your destiny!'

Mia looked into Bella's face. It seemed like every year showed in her worn, tired face, and she looked frail and vulnerable. Mia was torn. She didn't know what to think, or say, or do any more. A part of her wanted to spend the rest of her life with Trig and the other dragons, learning the old woman's secrets, becoming a magician, and yet another part of her just wanted to be an ordinary schoolgirl, growing up in Glenkilty and living a normal life with her family.

How had all this happened, that she had become so caught up with the old woman and lost touch with the real world? Perhaps she had read too many books and listened to too many stories, and somehow had led Bella to find her. The magic had overtaken her, her imagination guiding her to be here with Bella and the dragons. The whole thing was just so unbelievable that she couldn't think calmly and clearly about it at all.

'But what about my family, my Mum and Dad? I can't leave them Bella, I love them!'

'You will always love them, child, but you will not always stay their little girl. In time you will grow up, Mia, become a young woman and leave them anyway. Such is the way of life.'

An image of herself as a young woman flashed into Mia's mind – standing alone, power and magic filling her, looking down on a kingdom which she ruled.

The old woman stared deep into her eyes. 'You will have power, and knowledge of deep magic. Creatures great and small will bow down to your will and many will follow you, magician's daughter, believe me! You *want* to come with me, child. I know you do.'

Uncertainty crawled around Mia's brain, she felt the old woman was trying to control her thoughts and emotions. Instinctively, she looked away, concentrating on a small red robin that sat outside on the windowsill. Now she could sense Bella's annoyance. In an instant, the old woman had disappeared and Mia watched with horror as a huge, black cat sprang up on to the sill. The terrified robin, in a useless fluttering of wings, was tossed to the ground, and the self-satisfied cat crawled through the window and rubbed itself against her legs.

Glancing down at the cat's smooth, silky coat, Mia noticed the slightly raised marking on the cat's forehead which resembled dragon's wings, and realised that it was, in fact, Bella herself. Mia backed away, aghast, and watched as Bella changed back into herself again.

'I don't like interference,' she said sharply.

Mia was scared. What if Bella turned her into something and refused to turn her back again? The sorceress was staring at her intently, waiting for her reaction.

'When will you leave Glenkilty?' Mia asked softly.

'Tomorrow, perhaps, or the next night. When the wind is right and the moon is full, to guide us on our journey. You know we cannot delay much longer, child, or we risk the dragons being discovered. Can you imagine what your newspapers and television and radio would do if they found out about them! No, it's best that we leave for Dragon Wood and the castle as soon as possible. The dragons will be safe there.'

'What about Trig? He can't fly.'

'Aah!' said Bella, sighing 'Your favourite. Trig is a weakling, and besides, as you say, he cannot fly yet. How would I manage him along with the seven others? No, I will have to leave him behind.'

Hope swelled in Mia's heart. 'Let me mind him, keep him safe here with me,' she pleaded. 'I'll look after him, Bella, I promise.'

'Child, you know little of dragons. Trig would never survive here on his own. He is not a pet, like that little barking dog of yours. Trig is a dragon, one of the most complicated and rarest of creatures and, as you know, the blues are the most difficult to raise and train. Without the others, and left to survive in this modern world of yours, I'm afraid that Trig will die. It may take a few weeks, longer maybe, and I know those will be hard weeks for you as you are fond of him, but I'm afraid he will die.'

Mia didn't know what to say or do. Bella couldn't mean it,

just leaving Trig to die like that, pretending he didn't matter. Mia wouldn't stand for it!

'Take him with you! Take him to the castle too!' she pleaded. 'You can't just give up on him, he's such a beauty.'

'How can I take him?' the old woman shouted angrily at her. 'I have seven other dragons to mind, young dragons who have barely learned to fly and who have a long journey ahead of them. Do you want me to abandon them for the sake of one who is already weaker and injured and may not survive anyway?'

Mia shook her head.

'Come with me, child!' cajoled the old woman. 'You can carry Trig safely. He would travel with you, I know he would!'

Mia didn't know what to say. She suspected the old woman was manipulating her, using her love of Trig against her, but at this moment she felt she had no choice but to go.

'If I go with you, you must promise me that you'll let me return home when I want. Do you promise?' she insisted fiercely. 'I'm only going to help you with Trig and then I'll come back to Glenkilty! Promise that you'll set me free then!'

The old woman glanced down at the floor furtively.

'Promise!' insisted Mia, forcing the woman to look her in the eye.

'Aye, I promise,' said Bella slowly, her blue eyes seeming sincere and truthful.

Mia took a long, deep breath. She wasn't sure exactly what

lay ahead, but she couldn't deny the stirring feeling of excitement that rippled through her at the thought of being an apprentice magician and dragon keeper, even if it were only for a short time.

'Come, Mia, there is much for us to do before the moon has completed its full circle and our journey begins.'

Chapter 9

Stolen Child

Mia gazed up at the moon, which hung like a giant yellow cheese in the dark sky. She was confused by all that Bella had told her. She didn't want to leave her family, but what about Trig? There didn't seem to be any way out at all and she felt scared and weary just thinking about it. A part of her wished that she could climb into bed, fall asleep and wake the next morning to find that Bella and the dragons were gone.

She felt tense and nervous and didn't know what to do. She paced up and down her bedroom, trying to feel brave and excited and spirited, instead of sick and scared and weepy. She wanted to run away and hide. She wished Rory was there, but he was at the cinema with some school friends and wouldn't be home for ages.

Granny and her two best friends, Daisy and Ivy, were downstairs, playing cards and chatting. She'd sat with them for a while, sharing some of Granny's sponge cake.

'You look done in, Mia, pet!' Granny had remarked, and suggested that she go to bed early.

'The teachers make them work far too hard in school nowadays,' said Daisy Donovan. 'The child looks like a little white ghost after all that homework!'

Mia could hear their comforting voices below in the sitting room as they chatted the evening away.

She looked around her bedroom, loving every bit of it, her soft, squashy bed, her pine chest of drawers, so overloaded with clothes she could barely open or close them, the narrow corner wardrobe, her desk and chair and her shelf of books and knick-knacks. All ordinary and normal and wonderful. How could she leave them? She lay on the bed, waiting.

Rory came in. She heard his footsteps on the stairs. He pushed open her door to tell her about the film and say goodnight. She was tempted for a moment to tell him everything, but instead she rolled over on her side and pretended to be asleep. She waited and waited till she was sure her brother was sound asleep in his own room.

Bella had told her to come before midnight. Slipping on a pair of trainers and a tracksuit, she worked up the courage to creep across the landing, down the stairs and into the kitchen. Jackie looked up expectantly from her bed in the corner. Mia went quickly to the biscuit tin and bribed the dog with a chewy treat. Turning the key in the back door, Mia let herself out quietly into the moonlit night. She gasped. Bella was already standing there at the door amidst her mother's pots of daffodils and tulips.

'I knew you'd come, child!' she said, hugging her, and keeping her scrawny arms around her as they made their way back through the gap in the hedge.

The old house lay still and dark, most of the furniture and bric-a-brac already removed.

The dragons were quivering nervously with anticipation, and Mia was soon caught up in the excitement of what lay ahead and the great journey they would make together.

'Here, child!' said Bella. 'This is for you!'

Mia found herself being wrapped into a huge, feathered coat, her shoulders and arms being eased through enormous armholes.

'It's a flying coat, Mia! Rare and precious.'

The feathers felt soft and warm around her, feathers of every shape and size. She tried to guess the type of birds they had come from as she touched the shining blue-black feathers that covered her forearms, the grey seagull feathers that ran across her shoulders, and the soft, downy layers of pale white and silver that rippled along her midriff. Owl, thrush, sparrow, magpie, rook, blue-tit – she recognised many of them. Others were rich with strange colours and the exotic hues of birds that had never crossed the shores of her native land. It was magnificent.

'It's beautiful, Bella,' she said, caressing it. It fitted her perfectly, covering her whole body.

'Not many people have experienced flying, Mia. This

makes you truly special,' announced the old woman. She then slipped on a feathered coat of her own. The colours were darker, the plumage stronger, making her thin face and beady eyes look even more birdlike.

The dragons shoved and pushed each other anxiously, Bella moved amongst them, issuing commands in a low voice. Trig shuffled over beside Mia. The silence was suddenly disturbed by the urgent ringing of the front door bell. Bella looked startled, and in a flurry of temper went out into the hall.

✧ ◆ ✧

It was after midnight when Rose Murphy discovered that Mia was neither in bed nor anywhere in the house. In a panic, the old woman woke her grandson and they rushed outside. Luckily, her two friends had not yet left and were sitting chatting in Daisy's ancient Mini that was parked in the driveway. Rose was glad that she had already confided in them her misgivings about Bella Blackwell.

Rory raced out into the back garden, calling Mia's name, while the three old friends marched purposefully up the driveway to Bella's house.

'I'm sure and certain Mia is here!' proclaimed Rose, ringing the doorbell.

'Open the door, Bella!' she demanded. 'I know Mia is there with you! Give me back my grandchild this instant!'

'The poor child must be bewitched,' insisted Ivy Harrington, as the three elderly women stood on the front steps of The Elms, hammering at the wooden door.

'We must stop this Bella Blackwell woman,' added Daisy Donovan, her fat cheeks flushed with temper. 'Who does she think she is, stealing away your granddaughter, Rose?'

Both Daisy and Ivy had become very agitated, knocking again and again and peering in through the broad, front bay window of the old house.

'Let her find somebody else!' said Rose angrily. 'Mia is *my* grandchild!'

Much to their surprise, the heavy front door began to swing open, but there was no one holding it. They could see into the empty hall. They stepped cautiously inside, but there was no sign of Mia.

Bella suddenly appeared. She wore a strange coat which was layered with hundreds of fine, multicoloured feathers.

'A flying coat!' gasped Ivy.

Rose stood firm, facing the enemy. 'Give me back the child, Bella Blackwell, and that will be the end of it!' she demanded, her eyes flashing. 'She is entrusted to my care by her parents and I'll not let you harm her.'

Bella Blackwell moved menacingly towards them on her scrawny, birdlike legs. 'Then you should have kept a better eye on her, shouldn't you, Grandmother?'

Rose stared into Bella's eyes, reading the hatred there.

'Always the three of you together – I'm sorry that I cannot

entertain you,' she cackled wickedly and flew up in the air, up towards the ceiling just above their heads.

Rose grabbed a firm hold of the coat, sending two or three feathers floating to the ground. Bella laughed.

'Rose, Daisy dear, and Ivy, I do declare that I'm sorry we cannot sit down and be civil and have a nice cup of tea and a chat, but you know, I really must ... *fly*!'

'MIA!' screamed Rose Murphy at the top of her voice, the sound filling every corner of the old house.

But before Rose had a chance to repeat her granddaughter's name, Bella's spell took hold of her and she found herself lying ... stiff and thorny, covered in green leaves and fragrant pink blooms. Daisy had become a broad bush in full flower, and Ivy was transformed into a creeper, her tendrils curling along the ground, beside her friends.

✧ ◆ ✧

'MIA-A-A-A!' It was her grandmother's voice calling her, searching for her, trying to rescue her.

The seriousness of her predicament suddenly struck Mia and she tried to rush out into the hall, and call her granny's name. But no sound would come from her lips, no matter how hard she tried to shout and scream, and her legs would not move. She stood mute and still and miserable as Bella dealt with the three old women in her own way.

The sorceress returned, her coat flapping, her eyes like black coals.

'We must go immediately!' she said sharply, ignoring the tears that welled up in Mia's eyes. Petrified, the young girl followed her out through the open doors of the glasshouse and into the moonlight. Trig clung nervously to the inside of the huge pocket of Mia's coat where Bella had placed him. He looked squashed and uncomfortable, but did not protest.

Arznel and Oro had already taken to the sky and were circling impatiently over the house, black shadows crossing the moon. One by one, the others followed nervously.

'We are ready, child. Time to be gone! Fly!'

Mia felt the old woman's long fingers clutch her wrist and pull her up into the air, her feet lifting off the ground. Terrified, she looked down as her familiar world fell away below them – the grass and flower beds and bushes and roofs of the houses spinning dizzily away from her, as her arms and body moved in the unfamiliar rhythm of flight.

Chapter 10

The Flying Coat

They flew all through the night, guided by the stars. The flying coat moulded itself to Mia's body; her arms flapped up and down like wings and she was powerless to stop them, even though her muscles ached with exhaustion. She saw very little during the journey, conscious only of Bella's sharp words, the constant sound of beating wings and the sensation of cold air against her face and limbs as they journeyed ever onwards.

The dragons were lost in concentration too, trying to keep up a steady pace, not too fast or too slow, as they flew through the moonlight. As they tired, each took a turn to rest on the old woman's shoulder and let her fly for them. Mia was glad that Trig was squeezed tightly into the feathered pocket of her coat as she sensed that the young dragon was as scared as she was. Two of the female dragons, Flett and Frezz, flapped nervously alongside Bella, needing her constant guidance, and plummeting alarmingly every now and then.

Mia had lost all sense of time or place. Eventually, they began to slow down and circle, like wild swans or geese descending to earth. They flew lower and lower, heading towards a looming black shadow hidden in the depths of a large, dark wood, the twisted, crooked trees like deformed sentries guarding ... what? Mia wasn't sure. Was it a castle? She couldn't tell because the moon was hidden behind a cloud.

With an awful bump and thud she hit the ground, her wings becoming arms again, though not quick enough to prevent her from grazing her leg on the cold stone of a cobbled court-yard. Bella landed softly beside her, then guided the dragons down one at a time.

Mia clutched her bloodied knee and tried to get a look around at her surroundings, but it was too dark to see anything.

'Get up, child!' ordered Bella, pulling her to her feet. 'It's far too cold to be outside. We've had a long journey and must rest.'

Bella led the way towards an arched entrance, her feet moving quickly and lightly, sure of the way even in the dark. Tired and dazed, the dragons followed her across the court-yard. She herded them all into in a huge stone pen. Turning back, Bella crossed the courtyard again and opened a door which led to a drab entrance hall. She climbed a curving stair-way, with Mia stumbling along behind her. As they walked through corridor after corridor, dusty candles burst into flame as Bella touched them.

'Here you are, Mia! This is where you shall sleep.' Bella stopped suddenly and opened the door to a small, neat room, suddenly illuminated by flickering candles. A narrow bed, covered by layers of thick, woven blankets and soft, inviting feather pillows, stood against one wall. There was a high, arched window directly across from it and in one corner a small log fire began to glow.

'You must be tired, child.'

Tired was the very least of it. Mia had never felt like this before in all her eleven years. Her arms and legs and back seemed like wobbly jelly and she longed for sleep.

'Good night, Mia!' said Bella softly, closing the door of the room behind her as she left.

Alarmed at being left alone, Mia ran after her, only to hear the key turn in the lock. She tried to open the window but it was shut firmly and criss-crossed with heavy iron bars. She was a prisoner.

Sighing, she went over and sat on the bed. It was soft and springy. Taking off the feathered coat, she lay down and pulled the blankets up around her, taking in her new surroundings. This place was awful. It smelled damp and musty, as if nobody had slept there for a long, long time. Why, oh why had she ever befriended that strange old woman and believed in her? Tears welled in Mia's eyes as she remembered her blue-and-white gingham bedroom at home, filled with her toys and books and clothes, her family asleep in their rooms beside her.

Through her tears, she was suddenly aware of movement from the discarded flying coat thrown across a chair in the corner. Trig peeped out, his bright green eyes blinking.

'Trig!' she whispered.

The small blue dragon twisted and turned, trying to free himself from the entangled feathers. Then, for a few seconds, he remained totally still, his nostrils and long snout quivering as he sniffed the chilly air. After some consideration, he trotted towards Mia, his claws tapping on the bare floor. She patted the bed. 'Up, Trig! Up!'

The dragon jumped up on to the blanket beside her. She could see he was trembling, he was as scared as she was.

'It's all right, Trig. Don't be afraid!' she tried to reassure him. 'You can sleep on the bed tonight.' Her hand reached out to touch his leathery skin. 'You're cold, poor thing!' she said, pulling the blanket over him. 'This will warm you up.' The small dragon stared at her as she patted him, his skin growing warmer under her touch as he stretched out beside her.

'It's all right, Trig!' she said yawning. 'We're together, you and I, and I won't let anyone harm you.'

✧ ✦ ✧

When Mia woke the following morning, sunlight was stealing through the window. At first she didn't dare open her eyes, hoping that the journey and the castle were just a bad dream. She thought hard about her own home trying to make it real.

Finally, she opened her eyes and harsh daylight revealed her worst fears – Bella was standing at the foot of her bed, staring intently at her.

'I hope you are refreshed, Mia. You have been asleep for such a long time. I've brought you some milk and some fresh bread, just out of the oven. Time to be up! The sun is high in the sky and there is much work to be done.'

Mia sat up. With a heavy heart she realised that nothing had changed, she was in the same room and the same hopeless situation as the night before.

'Eat your breakfast and then dress yourself,' ordered Bella, 'I've left some warm clothes there on the chair for you. Come downstairs when you are ready and bring that dragon with you. You're spoiling him!'

Mia ate quickly. She hadn't realised how hungry she was. She gave a piece of the crust to Trig who snapped at it greedily, his sharp, white teeth sending crumbs all over the place.

The young dragon then closed his eyes and snuggled up beside her, ready to doze off again. Mia stretched and moved him out of her way. She'd better get up quickly if she didn't want to annoy Bella. A jug of water and a heavy washbowl stood on a small stand in the corner of the room. Half-filling it, she splashed water on her face and washed herself lightly. Trig watched her as she began to dress in the strange clothes left out for her. Her tracksuit had been taken away and the flying coat was gone. In their place was a heavy, dark green skirt that fell to her ankles, the material rough but warm, a cream linen shirt topped by a heavy, knitted over-vest of the same colour that laced up the front, and a pair of oatmeal-coloured stockings. But her own trainers were still there and she put them on, at least something was familiar. A bone-handled bristle brush and comb lay on the dark wood dressing-table and she pulled the brush through her long hair, which was full of tangles from her flight through the wind. Finally dressed, she opened the door and Trig jumped off the bed to follow her.

'Come on, Trig, we'd better go downstairs. We don't want to make Bella angry with us!'

Chapter 11

The Shadow Hound

By now, Rory was frantic with worry. He shouted Mia's name as he searched the garden and the road outside their house. He couldn't understand why she would have left the house at this hour of the night. Just as he was despairing of ever finding his sister, instinct and a strange sense of foreboding led Rory next door to The Elms. There was no sign of Granny or her friends anywhere.

'Mrs Blackwell! Mrs Blackwell!' he called out, ringing at her doorbell. There was no reply. Maybe she was already asleep in bed?

He walked around the edge of the house, peering in through the windows like a burglar. All the doors were locked. The house was totally dark, and seemed deserted. Rory began to panic, but he tried to stay calm, he needed to think. Where could Mia be? And where was Granny?

The glasshouse was in darkness too, the moonshine glittering on its panes. He noticed that the door was slightly ajar, so he pulled it open and stepped inside. Tall plants surrounded him, towering over his head. The air was full of a strange scent – lily, tomato plants, and something else, something he couldn't identity. He walked across the boards in the darkness, trying to feel his way, bumping into things, bruising his shins and hips, as he searched for the light switch. Eventually, he found it. He blinked as the bare bulb lit up the blackness.

There was no trace of anything unusual, just the normal contents of any old glasshouse. He was about to leave when he noticed a curved piece of hard shell lying at the edge of a large ceramic urn. Curious, he lifted it up. It shimmered black and green and turquoise. As he looked at it, turning it over in his hands, he suddenly realised what it was – a claw, some kind of animal claw. He stuffed it into the pocket of his jeans, then tried the door into the drawing room. It was open.

Silently he slipped into the house. He gasped – the room was almost empty except for the huge couch, and all that was left in the hall was a bunch of flowers and some plants that Bella must have knocked on to the carpet. He stepped over them. The kitchen, the dining room, the bedrooms – it was the same everywhere. The house was almost bare, with no trace of the old woman, or his sister, anywhere.

Rory sat on the bottom step of the stairs, his head in his hands. He didn't know what to do, but somehow he had to find Mia. Had the old woman taken her, spirited her away? He couldn't understand where Granny could have got to either, just when he needed her most. Rory decided to look for Mia first, then try to find Granny Rose. The woods seemed the most likely hiding place – he'd search there.

Racing back home, he threw on his hooded sweatshirt and flung a few things into his backpack and loaded new batteries into his torch. He left a note for Granny to say he was looking for Mia in the woods, and grabbed a bar of chocolate, a packet of crisps and filled a bottle with water, just in case he got hungry.

Now, where was Jackie? It struck him that it was strange that she wasn't barking or following him. He was crossing the front lawn, softly calling the dog's name, when he suddenly stopped in his tracks. A big, black shape stood on the grass in front of him. The menacing figure blocked his way, preventing him from climbing over the fence. It was a huge dog, a massive wolfhound-type, bigger than any dog he had ever seen before.

'Get out of my way!' Rory shouted, trying to keep his voice from shaking.

Something about the hound, the way he looked at him, put Rory at his ease. Like a whisper echoing in his mind, he suddenly, inexplicably *knew* that this creature could help him. But his thoughts frightened him – it was all too strange.

'Move!' he shouted again, trying to scare it away.

The huge hound pricked up its ears and turned its massive square jaw and head towards him. Unperturbed, it stared at him. Rory walked nearer and nearer to the hound, astounded by his own bravery, till he was almost touching its shaggy side. Looking into the deep brown pools of its eyes, Rory seemed to understand what it wanted. He knew that this huge hound did not intend to hurt or harm them. It had been sent to help him find Mia.

Aware that this was the craziest thing he'd done in his whole life. Rory took hold of the hound's long coat and clambered awkwardly onto its strong, broad back. Wrapping his arms tightly around the shadow's neck, twining his fingers through the thick grey-brown hair, he let the giant wolfhound take him away to search for his missing sister.

They began to move, the hound taking a massive leap and soaring over the garden fence. Rory clung on, his heart pounding beneath his ribs as the animal gathered speed and began to race through the narrow, overgrown paths of Glenkilty Wood. He ducked his head as branches and twigs scraped against him. Suddenly, he became aware that the ground seemed to be falling away beneath them and that the tall trees now danced under them. He felt dizzy for the first few minutes, and closed his eyes as the ground shifted giddily below. He hung on for dear life – and slowly got used to the strange sensation of flying.

Rory held on as tight as he could, trying to keep his balance and move with the sweeping glides of the hound as it swung over the village of Glenkilty. He could just about distinguish the spire of the church and the roof of the school. Higher and higher they went, leaving the village behind and flying into the swirling wind. He began to feel less and less afraid. He felt he could go to the ends of the earth now if he had to, to get Mia back. He could journey with this flying hound far, far away.

All night long they flew, Rory was barely awake when the early morning sunlight began to fill the sky. Exhausted, he leant against the dog, listening to the rhythm of its breathing, his head nodding as they flew lower and lower over a changing landscape.

Chapter 12

Bella's Castle

Mia looked around her at the old stone castle. The walls were covered in mould and the wooden beams were rotten and patterned with woodworm. The whole place smelt of dampness and of not having been used for a long, long time.

'This dampness is bad for the dragons. It gives them dragon cough. So we must get the place cleaned and opened up properly,' said Bella, fussing about. 'We don't want a lot of sick dragons on our hands!' She showed Mia around what seemed like miles and miles of drab, grey corridors and dusty rooms.

'Blackwell Castle was once the finest castle in Arbor, child. All the rest have crumbled and fallen away, lost and forgotten now. You'll see, the dragons will bring life back to this place. The sky will resound once again with the sound of dragons' wings, and magic will fill the air. Now, with the return of these dragons, the castle will regain its glory!'

Looking at the crumbling, moth-eaten velvet curtains and tapestries and the woodworm-infested furniture, Mia found it hard to believe in the castle's former glory.

'Those were the days! Good days!' sighed Bella. 'Heavens willing, they will return.'

They walked through a huge, neglected banqueting hall, the long timber table covered with mouse droppings.

'I can't remember the last time a feast was served in this room,' said Bella wistfully. She muttered something under her breath and, as they stood there, the room seemed to shift. Suddenly, a fire burst into flame, burning brightly in the grate. The table's polished surface gleamed in the light. Goblets of gold and silver sparkled on the table that was now heavily with laden with food of every description. A whole pig, a juicy apple stuck in its mouth, lay in the centre of the table. Music played softly in the background, the sound of unseen musicians. Then, just as quickly, the image disappeared and the room resumed its unwelcoming, neglected look.

'Come,' said Bella briskly, 'I will show you the courtyards!'

Mia and Trig followed her.

A whole series of courtyards encircled the outside of the castle. Some were open, others were covered by what looked like a mesh of heavy fishing nets.

'These are the training yards.'

Trig sniffed, as if he sensed that this was something that concerned him.

'We work under the nets at first and then later on out in the open. Each dragon is different and will have a training schedule of its own, although there will be group lessons too. You will learn, child!' said the dragon woman, squeezing Mia's hand. Bella looked tired. The journey had drained all the colour from her face and even her voice sounded weary.

'Let us go and say good morning to the dragons. They should be well rested after their journey by now.'

Some dragons lay sleeping in the sunlight, others sat, snouts pressed anxiously against the iron bars of the pens.

'Trig, this is where you were *meant* to sleep,' said Bella crossly, and ordered him inside, lifting the iron hatch. Mia could not believe how obedient Trig was – he did exactly what Bella told him. 'Remember, Mia, Trig is not a pet!'

Bella greeted each of the young dragons in turn, and Mia found herself hunkering down beside them, tickling one under the chin, rubbing the tummy of another, patting a shoulder and a forehead, Trig eyeing her jealously all the while. Bella watched her approvingly.

'I knew it, child! You were born to handle dragons. They like you and it is clear that you like them. It does my old heart good to see it. Come! We must go inside and prepare some food for them. They will also need fresh water.'

The kitchen seemed miles away. It had high, barred windows that looked out across a magnificent silvery blue lake, which formed a natural moat that surrounded the castle.

'Put that on, child! It will protect your clothes!' Bella said, tossing her an apron.

Despite her age, Bella moved quickly about the kitchen, pulling out pots and pans and filling them with all kinds of strange ingredients. Mia had to fetch food from the shelved pantry and from the cold room, which made her teeth chatter each time she went. Bella barked orders, 'Cut this! 'Chop that!' 'Peel this!'and Mia did as she was bid, watching steam rise from large, bubbling pots.

'Dragons are finicky creatures, picky eaters at the best of times,' complained Bella.' 'They need lots of nourishment to build up their strength.'

A strange, sour smell drifted from some of the pots, and when Mia stirred them it made her feel queasy. Yuck!

'I've sent Gwenda to get some provisions for us. We will eat later.' Bella didn't explain who Gwenda was and Mia was afraid to ask.

The dragons gobbled up the prepared food, licking their dishes and searching for more. Only Trig left his breakfast half-finished, staring at Mia with mournful eyes.

Bella set Mia to sweeping the floor and scrubbing the big kitchen table. She worked till her arms ached and her hands were covered with big blisters. There was just so much to be done. There was probably an army of servants and maids working in the castle in times gone by, she thought, no wonder it had fallen to such decay now.

'So, she's set you to work already, my girl!'

Mia looked up in surprise to see a broad, hefty young woman push in the kitchen door. 'Give me a hand, will you?'

Mia couldn't help staring at the strong face and the high, pointed eyebrows and funny turned-up nose of this strange girl. The girl threw her packages on the table and removed her heavy, green cloak. She grabbed an apron from a hook on the wall and pulled it on over her head.

'I do hate haggling and bartering, it always gives me a headache. Still, I reckon I got most of what the old one wants.'

Mia sat open-mouthed, unsure of what to say.

'I'd shut that mouth if I were you, my girl, or you might swallow a flying flea. The castle's full of them!'

'Sorry,' Mia mumbled.

'I'm Gwenda, by the way.'

'And I'm Mia.'

'You're Bella's new apprentice! I've heard much about you, magician's daughter.'

'And you? Who are you?'

'I told you already. My name is Gwenda, Gwenda Rowancroft. I am a dwelf.'

'Dwelf?'

'Part dwarf, part elf. You *have* heard tell of us, I presume!'

Mia shook her head.

Gwenda laughed in disbelief. 'You have a lot to learn, young Mia.'

At least Gwenda was kind and was prepared to help Mia. She spoke slowly and showed her every corner of the huge kitchen and how to use the cooking range.

'You will settle in, child, don't fear. Bella's not as bad as she seems. I cried for the whole of the first year that I came to work here, and that was many moons ago. Once you keep the old sorceress happy and do not cross her, all will go well, I promise.'

Gwenda kept Mia busy for the rest of the day and there was no sign of Bella till suppertime.

Despite the delicious warming chicken stew and fresh bread she'd helped to make, Mia kept yawning at the table.

'You'd best away to sleep, Mia child,' suggested Bella. 'We have an early start in the morning. The dragons themselves were tired today, but tomorrow morning we will begin training them.'

Half-asleep, Mia made her way back to her small bedroom, wishing that she was not so alone and that Trig was there with her. She had barely undressed when she heard a scratching and snuffling outside her door, and opened it to find the young dragon there. Pushing past her, he made a swooping leap for the comfort of her bed.

'Oh, Trig!' she said, hugging him tight, and wondering whether it was Gwenda or Bella who had been kind enough to let the young dragon keep her company. Exhausted, she fell into bed, glad of the warm bundle cradled across her feet.

She wondered how long the old woman intended to keep her in the castle, how long would she need her help. Feeling lonely and scared and homesick, she cried herself to sleep.

Chapter 13

Giants' Cave

'Aargh!' shouted Rory, landing with a crashing thud on the rough ground, as the huge hound came to a sudden halt, catapulting him over its shoulder. He rolled over in the dirt, hoping the animal wouldn't stand on him by accident with its huge paws. He sat, gulping air, trying to get his breath back, his ribs and side aching.

Where was he? The early morning air was chilly and he shivered, trying not to be afraid. At least the grass beneath his fingers was green, and the sky was turning from a dusky grey to blue.

'Where are we?' he demanded. 'Is my sister here, is that it?'

The hound stood, nose twitching, watching as the yellow sun warmed the sky and light began to ripple out over the surrounding fields. The hound nosed at his arms and shoulder and he patted it absentmindedly as he would pat Jackie, his own dog.

'Come on! You've brought me this far, show me where to go now!'

The massive wolfhound stayed resolutely still as the sun rose high in the sky. He began to whine restlessly, then, without warning, he took off at a gallop into the distance, leaving Rory there all on his own.

'Come back! Don't leave me!' Rory shouted uselessly.

He waited and waited, but the hound did not return. Finally, he stood up and surveyed the vast landscape. He decided he had to move on. Looking about him, Rory wondered what part of the country he was in – he had never seen such rich farmland, each field was bursting with crops and vegetables. Corn and wheat and rye reached to his elbows and shoulders, enormous fronds of carrot-tops and cabbages and onions burst from the ground. He'd never seen anything like it. The soil must be unusually fertile to produce such huge crops. He was glad of his water bottle, slaking his thirst as the sun beat down, burning his fair skin.

As he walked on he noticed a rusting rake flung into a potato patch. It looked strange, different, oversized. He passed field after field, wondering when he would come across a farmhouse or a village. Finally, he spotted a plume of smoke in the distance and some kind of stone-built settlement. Perhaps someone there might be able to help him.

Hiding in the long grass, he decided to watch and discover what kind of people lived here.

'Got you!'

Rory nearly died with fright at the booming voice. Then a long arm and big hand grabbed him and pulled him out of his hiding place. His heart thumped with fear and he struggled wildly to escape. It was a girl – a *giant* girl! At least three times his size! She held him firmly.

'Well, look what I just found for myself!' she laughed, poking him with her finger and prodding him like he was some sort of toy doll. 'Wait till Father sees what I caught today!'

Rory blinked. He didn't believe it. A giant standing before him – he was seeing her with his very own eyes. The girl bent down towards him excitedly. He tried to turn and run, but she blocked his escape, laughing at his attempt to get away from her. She had a big, round face and deep blue eyes and her long fair hair was in two thick plaits that hung like ropes on either side of her head.

'Boy! You *are* small!' she said, poking at him again with her finger, which felt like a thick tree-branch sticking into his ribs.

'Are you a dwarf?'

Rory stood up tall and straight. '*Me*? A dwarf?' he declared fiercely. 'It's *you* who's far too big!'

She began to giggle again. 'Thank you! That's a nice thing to say.'

'Where am I?' he asked, trying to keep the tremor out of his voice.

The girl wrinkled up her face and eyes, peering at him in disbelief. 'You're in Giants' Cave, of course,' she explained.

'Giants' Cave? Is this where my sister is? Have you seen her?

The giant girl looked puzzled. 'I have no idea what you are talking about, stranger.'

Keeping it simple he tried to explain about Mia's disappearance, while the girl sat on the ground listening to him.

'Birch!' A loud voice broke into his story and summoned the girl home. 'Come in here this instant, Birch, there's work to be done before your father arrives.'

The girl hesitated, and Rory knew that she was trying to decide what to do about him.

'Don't be scared!' she whispered reassuringly, lifting him off his feet and carrying him in through the cave entrance, along a stone passageway and down into the kitchen where her mother was busy attending to a huge range where pots boiled fiercely, filling the air with steam.

'Ma! Look what I found outside!'

The giant mother turned around quickly, and almost dropped the pot she was stirring.

'Oh, my! Birch, what is it? A nasty dwarf or a goblin of some sort? Take care, it might bite or scratch you!' she warned, coming closer to him to get a better look.

'He's a boy, Ma! A small sort of one, but he's a boy.'

'Be careful of him, Birch, there's no telling what he might do. You know you can't trust them. Your father's warned you often enough. Put that willow basket over him, then I can keep an eye on him till your father gets home.'

Rory sat totally still, the strips of the willow basket imprisoning him, as the giant mother and daughter worked at setting the table and filling a jug with a red berry juice and chopping raw vegetables into a huge bowl. They both wore shapeless grey dresses that at times almost camouflaged them against the grey stone wall of their home.

Birch placed a large loaf of fresh, crusty bread on the table, and Rory longed for a small piece of it to fill his empty stomach.

A short time later, Rory's heart nearly stopped beating with fright as the dwelling rumbled and echoed with the sound of huge heavy steps – Birch's father! The moment he entered the kitchen he spotted Rory and came over to peer at him.

'Where did you find him, Birch?' he asked his daughter anxiously. 'You didn't go out across the fields mouse-catching, I hope!'

She shook her head.

'There isn't a pick on him, is there?' said the giant. 'His legs and arms aren't even the size of chicken bones. He seems quiet enough too, not very fierce.'

Tears pricked Rory's eyes. Perhaps the giant was going to eat him, break every bone in his body with those huge teeth of his.

'Bran Bigg, look what you've done!' snapped his wife. 'The poor child is crying. You know I can't stand the tears of a child.' She plopped down on a heavy kitchen chair and blew her nose loudly.

'There, there, Bessie love, I didn't mean nothing by it.'

Rory wiped his eyes with his sleeve. These giants were certainly not like anything he'd expected. They seemed like gentle farm people, almost unaware of their immense size.

'Give the boy something to eat,' ordered the giant, pulling the stool up close by him at the table. Birch broke up a small corner of bread for Rory and her mother spooned out some thick stew which she placed on a small saucer in front of him. He didn't know what was in the stew, but he gulped it down anyway.

'He likes my cooking,' said the wife, tickling Rory's chin with her finger as if he were a baby, and insisting on giving him a second helping.

'Where does he come from, Da? How did he get here?'

Rory's mouth was so full of the rich gravy and vegetables that he couldn't reply.

'The boy will tell us in his own good time,' said her father.

'He said he's looking for his sister,' stated Birch. 'I wish I had a sister or brother,' she added wistfully.

'Birch Bigg, stop that nonsense! You know well that a giant family is always just a Ma and Da and a little one, always has been and always will be. That's the giants' way.'

Birch looked crestfallen.

Her mother gave her a warning glare and Birch busied herself pouring out the juice into the heavy glass goblets on the table. Rory was given what looked like an earthenware eggcup to drink from.

'What's your name, boy?' asked the giant, crunching on a huge piece of raw celery.

'Rory.'

'Rrroorrie. 'Tis strange sounding.'

'Rory Murphy.'

'Murrffee,' repeated the giant. I have never heard tell of any of your folk. Are you part dwarf or goblin, or more human?'

'All human,' said Rory firmly.

'That's a shame,' murmured the giant, 'a crying shame.'

Rory gulped the strong-tasting juice and said nothing.

They ate the rest of the meal in silence, and every now and then Rory glanced at the girl to try and ascertain what might happen. Birch concentrated on eating and would not return his gaze at all. Afterwards, Birch and her mother cleared the table and Birch's father produced a large pipe which he filled with tobacco, and began to smoke. He lifted Rory up and placed him on a chair beside him.

'Now, boy, I've been patient with you, more than patient, you must agree. Tell me how you came to Giants' Cave. Have you been sent to spy on us, is that it?'

Rory shook his head. 'No sir! Honestly – no!'

'How did you get here, then? Those short little legs of yours couldn't carry you within miles of here!'

'A huge hound that could fly through the sky carried me here. I don't know how the hound found me or why he left me here in Giants' Cave,' replied Rory.

The giant leaned forward his eyes wide, 'The Shadow Hound,' he breathed. 'That was the Shadow Hound. 'You have really *seen* him?'

'Yes, sir, I rode on him! He was the one who brought me here.'

Rory stared into the fire, wondering if the giants would believe his far-fetched story or just decide to tear him limb from limb, or whatever giants did to unwelcome guests.

'I am searching for my sister, Mia. She disappeared from home, kidnapped by a crazy old woman from next door,' he confided, hoping they would believe his far-fetched story. 'It was the hound who brought me here. We flew all through the night searching for Mia, but there is no sign or trace of her, and then when the sun came up that stupid dog just took off and left me stranded here. I don't know what I'm going to do! I'll never get Mia back from Bella Blackwell. I'll never find her!' he sighed hopelessly.

Birch had come over and was sitting on the arm of her father's chair. 'You *saw* the Shadow Hound, *rode* on his back! Da, did you hear that?'

The giant nodded, puffing slowly on his pipe. 'Times are changing, the Huges and the Longs have been saying it for some time. I've heard tell of the great Shadow Hound, of course, but we have never actually seen him.'

'He was outside our house back home in Glenkilty, waiting for me, and somehow I just knew what the creature wanted me to do.'

'So you rode with him!' gasped Birch, her eyes shining.

'Bella! Who's this Bella, then?' asked Birch's mother, wiping her hands on her apron.

'Mrs Blackwell is an old lady who moved into the house next door to us. My mum said that we should be neighbourly, be nice to her. I used to call her the Bird Woman but Mia said that she was a Dragon Woman, that she kept dragons, baby dragons. I didn't believe her,' he blurted out breathlessly. 'I told her she was imagining it! Why didn't I listen to Mia? Why didn't I do what my granny told me and mind her? She was so scared ... none of this would have happened if I'd only–'

'Hold on now, young man, your words are running away with you. Calm down!' urged the giant's wife.

'*Dragon*, did you say?'

'Yes. Mia said she saw them in Bella's house.'

The giant drew in his breath, taking a strong puff of his pipe. 'I haven't heard tell of dragons for many years, centuries even. They were all killed, destroyed, though there were always rumours that some had survived and gone into hiding – much like ourselves. Dragons, fancy that! Perhaps the old ways have not disappeared altogether, no matter what the Great Mage may have said or done.'

Rory couldn't make much sense of this, but before he could ask the woman butted in. 'Why has this Bella woman stolen your sister?'

'I don't know,' said Rory miserably. 'Mia thought that Bella was just a lonely old woman and tried to be her friend. She wanted Mia to be some sort of an apprentice and learn about dragons!'

'I wish I had a dragon,' sighed Birch.

'Birch!' Her mother sounded shocked. 'Are you wishing yourself spirited away by some nasty witch or sorcerer? Sorcery is behind this, mark my words!'

The giant got to his feet and went to a heavy bookshelf above the fireplace. Pulling an ancient-looking book from the middle of a row of books, he lifted it down, and, sitting down again, he began to turn over the heavy parchment pages.

Rory could read the title on the spine. *The Giant Chronicles.* He watched as Birch's father turned over page after page.

'Here it is!' he said at last, stopping and lowering the book to the floor.

Rory clambered down off the chair and knelt down on the fireside rug to get a glimpse of what Bran wanted to show him.

One side of the page was covered with pictures of dragons, flying wings outspread. On the other side of the page, written in red ink were the words: The History of the Dragon Wars.

The giant stabbed his finger at the picture.

'Look close, boy!'

Rory studied the drawing. It showed fire flaming from the mouth of an enormous black dragon, and although it was only a picture, he could see the glint of anger in his eyes. Behind him perched a crowd of smaller dragons. But it was only as Rory bent closer that he was able to make out the strange figure standing amongst them. He blinked, unable to believe what he saw there. It was Bella Blackwell, there was no doubt about it. Her face was almost hidden by a swirling black cloak, but he could still recognise her.

'It's Bella!'

'Aye,' said the giant, 'that's what I thought!'

Birch almost knocked her father over, trying to get a look, and even the giant's wife peered at it closely.

'I've got to find Mia,' declared Rory. 'She's caught up in something dangerous. This proves it.'

'You're right, boy. I'll call a meeting at Giants' Cave,' said Bran Bigg seriously. 'Someone may be able to help you in your quest. But now you look tired, tonight you must get some rest.'

Chapter 14

The Journey

Rory slept fitfully, curled up on a cushion in the corner. His mind was in turmoil, giants and dragons and witches all haunting his dreams, terrifying him. How had he fallen into this strange world? What had Mia got him involved in? There was no sense or logic to any of this. It was as if everything he had refused to believe in had suddenly come to life, challenging him.

He had managed to sneak a look at a few more pages of the book, which had given him some idea of the giants' history. They seemed a gentle people who had farmed and worked hard for centuries, creating a fertile land for themselves. Then things changed, and war came. The giants were used as weapons, striding into battle in heavy armoury, or used as carriers to bring other soldiers to the front. Many seem to have died that way judging by the illustrations in the *Chronicles*. The pictures changed as giants became the slaves of men, used to build castles and forts and temples and monuments. Families were destroyed. Rory was saddened by what he read and saw. Only a few giants survived, crossing deep swamps and hiding in the grey mountains and hillsides, blending with the caves and rocks which became their refuge and their home. Here they took to tilling the soil once again. It was a sad but honour-able history.

When he woke, the book was gone, deposited back on the high shelf where it would be impossible for him to reach it without a ladder.

The giants were very kind to him and took care of him well. Bran proudly showed him their farmlands, where giants laboured in the rolling fields and hillsides, tending their crops. Rory was amazed to see tomatoes the size of footballs, runner beans like green moving chains that clambered up huge canes towering above him, and apples like heavy, green cannon balls.

Birch followed him around, prattling on and on, reminding him of his sister. She insisted on showing him off to a group of shy friends, as if he was a new toy. Her friends' shyness soon gave way to curiosity and they quizzed him about his country.

When they left, he asked Birch if she had a map of the region.

She obliged him by unrolling a huge map across the kitchen table.

Rory walked across the map, from one corner to another, trying to make any sense of it. Birch's chubby finger pointed out Giants' Cave where she lived. Rory tried to memorise the geography of the region spread out before him.

'What is this?' he asked, pointing to the word *Terra* written in the top right-hand corner of the map.

'That is where *we* are! Our farms and lands are part of the territory they call Terra,' she replied.

'What lies beyond?'

She shrugged. 'Swamps and forests, the deep woods. I have only heard tell of them – the other territories.'

She blushed deeply, and he could tell that she thought she had said too much.

Rory sighed. So this was only a small part of it. There was still much he needed to learn.

The sky outside the cave was dark and the night was cold. Frost covered the ground and Rory's breath almost froze as he walked along beside Birch. Huge figures formed a semicircle on the dark hillside, where the giants were gathered around a glowing fire. One giant face after another turning to stare at him as he approached.

''Tis the boy!' Bran drew Rory into the circle of enormous men, women and children. 'This is Roree Murfee, a human. The Dragon Woman has taken his sister, spirited her away!'

A rumble of gossip rippled round the fire at the mention of the Dragon Woman.

'But the Dragon Woman died hundreds of years ago with all the dragons – every Giant knows that!' insisted a man with a mane of roaring red hair and a long beard. 'The boy must be mistaken.'

'Longbeard Huge, you do well to express your doubts, but the boy recognised the Dragon Woman in our *Chronicles* only a few days ago.'

'The dragons are dead, sky protect them,' murmured a huge woman who towered over Bran Bigg. 'Good ones and bad ones, all gone.'

'His sister saw dragons, only babies mind you,' interrupted Birch's mother. 'She told the boy about them but he didn't believe her, more's the pity! The Shadow Hound brought him this far, so I reckon the least we can do is help.'

A mutter of disbelief and objections filled the air.

'I saw a dragon!'

Everyone turned to see who had spoken.

'I saw a dragon, a black one, flying skywards out beyond the Boundary two days ago,' declared a plump-faced boy about Rory's own age.

'Why did you not tell someone, young Nilo?'

The boy giant looked nervously across at his father, Long-beard. 'Because I knew no one would believe me and I'd get into trouble.'

'Trouble?'

'Aye, trouble, for not being at school and for going outside the Boundary.'

'What was this dragon like?' asked an elderly giant who was sitting near the fire and toasting some bread for himself.

'At first, I thought it was just some kind of strange bird blown off-course. But it cast a black shadow across the ground, and when I saw that, I knew what it was. It was definitely a dragon! I was scared. I ran and hid in an old ruin till it flew past.'

'So, there be dragons again!' said an ancient giant who balanced on crutches made of two tree trunks. His head was covered in wispy white hair and his front teeth were missing. 'And the sorceress, Bella, has returned and will regain her powers, and she will try to rule the four territories of Aland! She will use the dragons to quell resistance. Her magic will grow more powerful, day by day. We giants may be in grave danger.'

'Bran says it was the Shadow Hound who brought the stranger here,' said the ancient giant, looking around the campfire. 'We should remember that it was the noble Shadow Hound who also brought the first giant across the filthy swamps, when he lifted Hugo Long from the battlefield where he had been left to die and brought him to the safety of Giants' Cave many years ago. He has now brought the boy to us, perhaps to warn us, or simply knowing that we would help him!'

'Aye! We should help the boy!' agreed a chorus of voices. 'We owe it to the Shadow Hound.'

The giants talked long into the night, devising a plan to take Rory to where the dragon had been seen. Bran Bigg would go with him, and young Nilo would lead the way.

Chapter 15

The Swamp

Before they set off the next day, the giant's wife served them an enormous breakfast of porridge, crumpets, honey and cherry juice. She filled Rory's backpack with food for the journey: a dried fish, some oatmeal biscuits, strips of charred beef, baby potatoes and a human-sized loaf of fresh bread that she had baked early that morning especially for him. There was also a flask of spring water and a sealed pitcher of juice. Birch cried all morning, begging him not to go.

'Stay with us here, Rory, and I could be your sister!' she pleaded.

Rory shook his head, thinking of Mia and how scared and alone she must be.

Birch squeezed him tight as he was leaving, and he almost felt dizzy!

'What about a hug for me?' Nilo teased Birch. Birch blushed deeply, as usual.

Eventually, all the farewells were made and it was time to leave Giants' Cave. Bran led the way down the hillside. Rory slipped and stumbled as the heavy rocks and stones moved beneath his feet. He was thankful for the giant boy beside him, who many a time lifted him up off the ground and stopped him from falling. He knew that he was slowing them up. But soon they reached the acres of green pasture land. They walked along, sometimes talking, sometimes not. They told him about the giant families – the Huges, the Biggs, the Longs, the Talls, the Stouts – and he in turn told them about his world, about his mother and father and Granny Rose, and the house they lived in, and all about Glen-kilty. They shook with laughter when he tried to tell them about television and computers, and called him a liar when he informed them about aeroplanes and cars.

'We don't believe you, lad. Nobody or nothing could send two hundred people flying through the air, unless it were witchcraft or high magic!'

Rory decided it was pointless trying to impress them any more about modern times.

They walked for hours, eventually stopping because he had to rest. His legs and feet were aching and the terrain was getting worse.

'Let me carry you, lad!' offered Bran. 'I used to carry Birch on my shoulders up to a few years ago, and, sure, you're no load at all.'

Bran knelt on the ground and Rory clambered on to his broad shoulders, gasping with fear when the giant stood up. He clasped Bran's head as the ground swayed beneath him.

'You hang on there, Rory lad!'

Bran and Nilo began to take larger strides now. A vast distance was covered in no time. They only began to slow down as the ground became heavy and muddy.

'It's the swamp!' announced Nilo, both giants stopping to look across a vast lake of thick mud.

'What'll we do now?' asked Rory, as there seemed to be no way to cross it.

'We wade,' said Bran firmly, stopping to take off his boots and strip off his trousers. Nilo followed suit.

Rory was terrified. He had read about such swamps in the *Chronicles* and he knew how dangerous they could be. He would suffocate in seconds if he fell into the mud.

Bran was silent as he entered the swamp, the mud squelching and gurgling between his toes. The ooze crept up his legs as he began to wade – to the knees, then to the thighs, then above his backside and up beyond his waist. It clung to his skin, trying to force him to stop walking. Nilo followed beside them, the ooze right up to his chest. Rory could see the fear in the other boy's eyes, and prayed that they would all make it.

They were right in the centre of the swamp when Bran

lurched. Rory shook wildly as the huge giant seemed to go down on one side, the ooze sticking to his chest and neck and spattering his face. Rory's own shoes and trousers were now mud-covered too.

'Hang on!' warned Bran.

Nilo moved slowly towards them and with his free arm pulled Bran free. Together, they stumbled out of the hole Bran had stepped into.

Exhausted and filthy, they eventually made it to the other side, where they lay on the ground trying to get their breath back.

'We should build a bridge over that filthy swamp!' muttered Nilo. 'I'm fed up having to go through it.'

Bran looked up at the boy. Why hadn't the giants thought of that before? There were enough of them to build a bridge if they put their minds and strength to it.

'You have a wise head for one so young, Nilo. We will raise it at the next gathering.'

The sun dried the mud on their skin and clothing, and finally, feeling more rested, they began to walk again.

'What I need is a good hot bath!' sighed Bran.

'You won't get that,' said Nilo, 'but I promise, soon we will be able to wash ourselves.'

They trudged on for another hour and then came to a sudden halt. Bran lowered his shoulders so that Rory could jump down.

A tumbling waterfall glittered and sparkled in front of them. They tested the water with their hands and it was ice cold.

'It must come from deep within the mountain,' said Bran. 'It will invigorate us, but we should light a fire first so that we can warm and dry ourselves afterwards.'

The three of them quickly gathered sticks and branches, piling them high, then Bran took a bronze tinderbox from his waistcoat and, with a few breaths, blew it into flame. They had a fire lit in no time. Then, stripping off their muddied clothes, their bodies caked in stinking ooze, Bran and Nilo ran under the freezing waterfall. The giants were shouting and enjoying themselves, as he would have enjoyed a hot shower at home, but he was glad to crouch at the fire and warm himself.

Bran and Nilo produced a handful of huge potatoes which they roasted in their jackets, sprinkling them with salt. The waterfall provided them with an iced drink. They sat till the night drew in, safe in the comfort of the fire.

'Tomorrow we reach the end of the Boundary,' said Nilo, taking a bite from his roasted potato, 'and we may get to see the dragon I told you of.'

Exhausted and bone weary, Rory fell asleep, glad of the giants' snoring on either side of him driving away the strange sounds that came from the darkness.

Chapter 16

The Dragon Keeper

All eight young dragons were eager and excited when they were finally let out into the largest open courtyard. They stretched their wings and lashed out with their long, pointed tails. The rays of the sun warmed them, and the dragons' skin sparkled like precious jewels in the light. They whined and yelped and made chirping noises, enjoying their freedom. Bella stroked and scratched them, her eyes filled with a strange excitement. Mia followed behind her.

'Now, listen! Listen well,' said Bella sternly. 'There are important lessons to be learned today!' Mia was unsure whether Bella was talking to her or to the dragons, though they all quietened down immediately.

Bella moved among them, slowly inspecting their wings and muscle tone and strength.

'As you already know, Mia, dragon wings are highly sensitive, and are all too easily injured or torn, taking weeks to heal.

That is why it is important for a good dragon keeper to check her dragon before letting it fly. The loss of even one dragon is too much!'

Mia nodded in agreement.

'Also, that is why it is so important for the young dragons to learn to take off and land and swerve safely, without injuring themselves.'

The old woman called the first dragon forward. Arznel was already much stronger and bigger than the rest.

'Arznel, you will lift off slowly, westwards from the parapet, and fly around the castle. Circle it twice, follow the line of the lake below us, then drop slowly and land. I will guide you down.' Bella whispered something into Arznel's ears and the powerful, young, black dragon began to run, gathering speed. He moved heavily, reminding Mia of an ungainly swan, his huge wings flapping up and down awkwardly, before taking off smoothly.

He flew away from them, then turned, his gleaming wings at full stretch as he circled high above their heads. They watched him as he flew up and up, almost to the top of the castle, and swung out into a wide circle.

Arznel was a powerful flyer, and Mia could tell that he was scouting his new surroundings. Finally, he began to drop down, slowing gradually until he landed perfectly in front of Bella.

'He's a natural flyer, Mia, just look at his wingspan and the way he holds himself.'

Mia had never seen anything so powerful and magical as Arznel. He was a handsome young dragon. Dink was next. He was a green dragon, and of a shorter and stouter build. Bella tried to encourage him, but it took at least five attempts before he managed a shuddering takeoff.

'Look skywards! *Skywards*!' ordered Bella, as he immediately began to lose height and drop towards them. With great effort, Dink managed to right himself and landed without injury. Rana, a medium-sized green, was next, taking wing easily.

'Are you watching, Mia? See how Rana is leaning too far to the left, she must correct it without losing speed.'

Mia loved the magical sound of dragon wings as they filled the courtyard. They took off one after the other, all doing their best to please Bella. Trig came to stand close to Bella snuffling at her hand for attention. But Bella ignored him. He wasn't ready to fly yet and had to content himself with just watching the others, learning from their mistakes. Strength and courage gleamed from the emerald-green of his eyes, and Mia sensed that he would make a good flyer yet.

All morning the dragons repeated the exercise, taking turns to fly and land. Bella suggested that Mia take a turn at instructing them.

'They must get used to your voice, Mia child! Don't be afraid!'

It was an incredible thing to stand there, directing a magnificent young dragon in flight. Her eyes were glued to every move until each landed safely back on the ground.

'Listen to me, child! Watch the dragons. You must learn to understand them, read their minds, so that in time you will be able to guide and control them.'

Mia found that if she really concentrated, she could almost see what the dragons saw as they circled the castle. The connection between them was so strong, she could sense their nervousness as she guided them down safely.

By lunchtime they were all exhausted and ravenous, and Mia was grateful for the big meal prepared by Gwenda. The dragons would rest for the afternoon, but Bella insisted that Mia join her in the library to study astronomy and astrology.

'To become a dragon keeper and apprentice mage, you will need to develop a broad background in many subjects, including the sciences,' she explained.

Bella took down charts that showed her the positions of the planets and the stars and the various configurations. It was a lot for Mia to learn and remember.

'I was only a wee bit of a girl, no more than three or four, when my mother began to teach me about dragons,' confided Bella. 'They say the younger an apprentice is, the better, magician's daughter. All my long life I have worked with and trained dragons and, truth to tell, I know of no other way of life, and do not wish to.'

'But there's so much to learn, to understand,' Mia pleaded.

'That was exactly how I felt when Dracon, the druid and Great Mage, took me here to this castle for training. You will learn, Mia. I will teach you everything I know,' promised Bella, hugging her gently.

'I love the dragons, Bella, you know that, but soon I will be returning home. Remember, you promised me!'

A look of ugly spitefulness crossed the old woman's face and her hand squeezed at Mia's neck, two fingers pressing against her throat, almost choking her.

'You are a guest in my castle, child! You would do well to remember that! Attend to your studies, I have work to do.'

Mia gasped, as the old witch woman stomped out and closed the library door firmly behind her. She couldn't understand it, at times Bella was caring and loving and kind to her, brushing her hair, giving her extra feather pillows for her bed, fetching her warm drinks and helping her, but today she had scared her. Was Bella someone she should fear or someone she could trust? It was so hard to know.

Trying to concentrate, she learned off the patterns of stars that shaped the Great Bear, the Little Bear, the Plough, drawing them out on a piece of paper to help her remember them. The thought of Bella's anger frightened Mia more than anything else, for there was no telling what the powerful old woman would do. And Mia was her captive, with no way of escape.

Chapter 17

The Boundary

Rory and the giants woke with the sun's rays warming their faces. They gathering up their things and began to walk. Rory noticed that he found this terrain easier, the overgrowth less dense, and the trees around him, though still towering above him, more of a height that he was used to. Bran's heavy feet awkwardly squashed bushes and hedgerows as he strode through them.

Nilo seemed alert and tense, every now and then his pale blue eyes glancing upwards to the clear, blue, unclouded sky.

'What is it Nilo? Are we getting near?' Bran asked.

The boy giant shrugged, and seemed fearful and uncertain. Both giants, in fact, were uncomfortable and unused to the new surroundings.

'We must leave you soon, Rory, as we are already within the territory of Arbor, the place of woods and forests. We call it Dark Wood. This is not our domain and we could injure

ourselves in such close confines,' said Bran gently, the branch
of a tree almost sticking into his eye.

'We should warn him of what lies ahead,' blurted out Nilo,
and Rory noticed a worried look pass between the giants.

'Be careful, lad!' warned Bran. 'Dark Wood is full of all
sorts of dangers, wild things that would attack a stranger.
Wolves and twisting snakes that lurk in the ground and stinging insects that can kill a man in a few seconds, and those
funny-looking beasts they call creepers!'

Rory was puzzled – he had no idea what a creeper was.

'Creepers are nasty things with a fierce bite,' warned Nilo.
'They look small and harmless with their big, soft eyes and
twitchy noses and tails, but they're vicious. Keep away from
them!'

In the valley below them, Rory could see a vast forest, a
small river wound its way lazily through the dense undergrowth.

'That forest below is most likely crawling with them,'
added Nilo.

Something moved silently above the forest, bigger than
any bird. Nilo began jumping up and down with excitement,
pointing.

''Tis a dragon! I told you I saw one!'

'Hush, boy!' warned Bran. 'Do you want the dragon to hear
you?'

They all watched as the dark shape circled over the tree
tops. It flew round and round, then rose upwards, gaining

height, heading in their direction.

The young dragon flew steadily, each wing moving in rhythm as it searched the area.

'We must hide!' warned Bran. 'Or else it'll hear, or see, or *smell* us! They say a dragon can smell people a mile off.'

He pulled the two of them in under the cover of a thick bush. As the dragon flew overhead, it threw back its head and gave a piercing cry, which almost froze Rory's blood in his veins. They could hear the heavy flapping of its black wings, stretched taut over its bony frame, as the dragon circled overhead.

'It smells us,' whispered Bran. He drew his pipe from his pocket and, using the tinderbox, set the tobacco alight. Puffing deeply, he let the strong scent of tobacco waft around them. The dragon passed overhead again, uncertain now, flying so low that Rory could see the deep veins and patterns on its skin. It sniffed with curiosity and disdain at the smell of the tobacco. The dragon's eyes gleamed brightly, then, with a last searching look, it rose high into the sky again and flew away from them.

'Sky protect me, but there be dragons still!' gasped Bran. 'I never thought I would live to see the day that a dragon would fill the sky.'

Rory sat on the grass, stunned into silence. He couldn't believe it! An *actual* dragon. He'd seen it flying with his very own eyes. Fantasy come to life, and here he was stuck right in the middle of it all! Poor Mia must be terrified out of her wits.

He was determined to go down into the forest immediately and continue his search for her. He stood up, ready to go.

'Hold on, young fellow my lad, don't be rushing to go down there yet or yon dragon might return. Take your time.'

They made their way down into the valley and Rory knew that the giants were now in great danger as they were visible from any distance.

'I'm sorry, Rory, but Nilo and I must return to Giants' Cave,' Bran finally announced, ' though we hate leaving you here.'

Rory nodded, not trusting himself to speak, lonely already, fearful and wishing they didn't have to go. They shook hands solemnly.

'I hope you find your sister,' wished Nilo sincerely.

Bran lifted him up in his arms and squeezed him hard to say goodbye. He passed him a small, well-folded length of parchment.

'Birch drew out this map for you. She copied it from the *Chronicles* to give you some idea of the land you must pass through. 'Tis easy to get lost in those wild woods.'

Rory studied it. The girl giant must have spent hours drawing out the scaled-down, miniature version of the map, with boundary lines and landmarks clearly marked for him: Terra, Arbor, Montan and Mare all defined, each a separate territory, making up the geography of Aland.

'Thank you so much, both of you, for helping me, and for coming this far with me. Thank your wife and Birch too.'

The giants strode off back up through the valley and Rory watched until the two huge, lumbering figures were out of sight. He was now on his own, and knew that in the forest, somewhere, there really were dragons and if he found them maybe he would find his sister, too.

Chapter 18

Dark Wood

After a while, Rory set off into the wood. It was dark and gloomy there, and the canopy of treetops blocked the sun's light from reaching the ground. Now he knew why they called it Dark Wood. Every sound was muffled too, except for the regular panting of his own breath and the smooth thumping of his footsteps, he could hear little else. From afar, the occasional high-pitched call of a bird broke the eerie silence.

Nervous and lonely, he tried to pretend that he was out for a walk in Glenkilty Wood, heading along familiar paths. He was hampered by the enormous, snaking tree roots that twisted across the ground, and by the dense overgrowth of brambles and thorns that dogged his steps, slowing him down. All around him grew ancient oaks as big as ships, giant chestnuts and massive sycamores. There were no pathways or tracks of any kind, so he had to rely on guesswork and intuition to decide which way to go. His father had always told him to follow his instincts, jump in, and not be afraid. If he could find that dragon, then Mia was likely to be close by. Determined to be brave and rescue his sister, Rory began to sing and whistle, the sound filling the dead, empty air.

He stopped to rest, finding a warm, sunny spot, where young, green shoots pushed up through the earth, searching for the light. He ate some of the bread, suddenly realising how hungry he was. In the distance he heard the soft gurgle of a stream, he managed to track it as it wove its way through a labyrinth of roots and stumps and mossy banks. He refilled his water bottle, thankful that at least he wouldn't die of thirst, then splashed cool water on his face.

Rory hoped that he wasn't just walking round and round in circles. He regretted not joining the scouts, but then the Murphys had never been an outdoor type of family! He knew that he was ill-prepared and ill-equipped for this expedition, and despair filled his heart when he thought of Mia. She could never survive in this harsh world.

As he moved through the woods, he had a constant sensation of being watched, often glimpsing a movement in the ferns and bracken out of the corner of his eye. He flung some stones to scare away what ever it was. He was terrified that it might be one of those creatures that Nilo and Bran had warned him of. He quickened his pace, trying to lose his stalker.

Snakes slithered across his path, then disappeared rapidly into the dense undergrowth and rotting leaf-piles. Trying to avoid one of them, he stumbled over a jutting stump of black-thorn, wrenching his ankle and shin. The throbbing pain forced him to stay where he was for the night.

The next morning, birdsong woke him, reminding him of home, but on opening his eyes he quickly remembered where he was. He moved his ankle and leg gingerly. No damage seemed to have been done. Sitting up, he was taken aback to find a furry creature almost at his toes. It reminded him of Snowy, their white rabbit at home, though its fur had patches of speckled brown and it was far bigger than their pet rabbit. Its long ears pricked up as Rory moved, and he could see teethmarks on his shoelaces where its sharp, pointed, white teeth had been nibbling. He sat up, scaring it away.

'Shoo!'

The creature hopped back, its nose twitching and its big eyes looking at him like some sad little kid. Standing up, Rory brushed the mud and dirt off himself, the furry animal watching him all the time. Opening his backpack, he took out a crust of bread, but it had hardened so much that he could scarcely chew it. In a temper he flung the stale bread to the ground, trying to banish all memory of his normal breakfasts of pancakes or muffins or hot toast. The furry animal sniffed at the bread, disdainfully at first, then lifted it, squirrel-like, in its paws and began to chew it.

Rory started to walk, the thing hopping after him. Sometimes it would disappear and then he'd notice a flash of white in the undergrowth and it would be back again. He was glad of the company and it felt vaguely like having his dog, Jackie, along with him. At times, he thought he saw another flash of white and guessed that there might be two or three of them. Anyway, they seemed docile and harmless enough, and he had no reason to be scared of such gentle, rabbit-like, animals.

Rory stopped to study Birch's map, trying to hazard a guess as to where he was and how far he had come. Green lines criss-crossed everywhere, illustrating the density of the woods, but gave him few clues as to his whereabouts. He put the map back in his backpack and retrieved a last precious square of chocolate to give him some energy.

The furry animal had become more daring now and had begun to chew on the tip of his trainers. He shook his foot to deter it, but the creature clung giddily on to his leg. Putting his hand down, he attempted to push it away. Suddenly, a sharp pain seared through his fingers, jolting his nerves. It had bitten him! The sharp, white teeth were still stuck deep in his skin.

'Ow! Ow! Get off! Get off!' he screamed in panic, as the animal bit down even harder on his finger. Rory noticed with horror that two other creatures were hopping forward to join the first.

Vvrrruunngg!

From nowhere, an arrow flew through the air. Rory jumped as the animal's grip instantly weakened, and, squealing with pain, it slumped to the ground.

'Killed it!' came a triumphant shout.

The other animals took off through the trees. Rory winced with pain, and saw that his two middle fingers were bleeding.

'Let me see that, stranger!'

Rory turned to see a boy, a bit older than himself, standing behind him, his bow still in his hand, a quiver of arrows slung across his back.

'Filthy things, those creepers! Let me see the bite!'

Still shocked, Rory tried to move his hand slowly, letting the stranger, with his plaited, jet-black hair and piercing brown eyes, examine it.

'It needs some salve, but since we've none we'll just have to wash it clean.'

Rory watched as the young archer poured water from a flask on to the wounds and then, pulling a piece of cloth from around his neck, covered the fingers.

'Thank you,' he said, still feeling shaky.

The other boy just nodded. 'I'm Conrad,' he said.

'Rory. Rory Murphy.'

They shook hands, each sizing the other up.

'I thought that creeper thing was going to bite the finger off me.'

'Would have done, too,' agreed Conrad, showing him his own hand with half his little finger missing.

'God!' said Rory, feeling sick.

'Never let one of those stupid-looking creepers get too close to you. I've heard of men getting their ears and noses bitten off!' warned Conrad.

Rory could feel the boy's brown eyes staring at him.

'You are not from these parts. What brings you to Dark Wood?'

'I'm searching for my sister,' Rory explained.

'So! A quest to find a fair lady.'

'Mia's just a kid, she's only eleven!'

'Run off into the woods, did she? Silly girl!'

'No! It's not like that! Not like that at all! Mia was kidnapped … oh, I don't know what you'd call it!' he said desperately.

'No doubt a band of thieves or vagabonds, hoping to hold her for a hefty ransom?' exclaimed Conrad.

Rory shook his head. 'I know who took her! It was Mrs Blackwell, a weird nutcase of an old woman who moved into the house beside us in Glenkilty. She wouldn't leave my sister alone, filling her head with nonsense about magic and dragons – all sorts of weird stuff. We should have done something to stop the evil old Bird Woman getting such a hold over my sister, but now it's too late, and Mia has disappeared!'

'Bird Woman? Blackwell? Did you say the name Blackwell?' A look of deep concern filled Conrad's eyes. 'You don't mean Bella, the Dragon Woman? She has many names and can take many forms, so legend says. Witch, wizard, sorceress, druid – she can be all things to all people. There were rumours years ago that she had passed on, but yet you say that you and your sister have seen her?'

'Yes.' Rory nodded miserably. This sounded even worse

than he had thought.

'How many comrades go with you on this quest?'

'None,' replied Rory truthfully. 'I'm alone!'

'*Alone*!' jeered Conrad. 'How well do you know these woods?'

'I have a map.'

'A map! Much good that will do you when a creeper attacks you or a swarm of stinging moths covers you, or a bloodsucking bat attaches itself to your scalp. Rory, my friend, there's danger all around you.'

Rory exploded in anger and frustration. 'What else can I do? Give up? Forget about Mia?' he shouted, pushing the other boy out of his way.

'Hold on there!' replied Conrad, grabbing Rory's arm. 'I'm just saying that we must be mighty careful dealing with the Dragon Woman, if we're to have any chance of rescuing your sister.'

We! Conrad had said we. Did that mean he was going to help? Hope filled Rory's heart.

'You'll help me?' he asked tentatively.

'Aye!' nodded the dark-eyed boy. 'After some consideration, I have decided to join you on this quest.'

Rory thanked his new friend, though he wondered why Conrad had really joined him. What reason did the other boy have for getting involved? He hoped that he could trust this new friend more than the soft-eyed, fluffy creature that had nearly bitten his fingers off only an hour ago.

Chapter 19

The Good Pupil

Mia learned more and more about the dragons with each day that passed. Oh, how she loved to watch them fly, see them getting braver and stronger. Arznel and Rana and Oro soared confidently over the woods that lay below the castle. Flett, Frezz and Gosha needed a little more patience and understanding, but in time they too would master the sky.

'Bella, when do you think Trig will be able to start flying with the others?' she asked, concerned for the young dragon who, she sensed, felt left out and neglected.

'It will be weeks before the blue is fit for anything, Mia!' Bella replied disdainfully.

Mia didn't dare argue with her, but even to her inexperienced eye Trig seemed much better. Still, Bella was the judge, the expert.

One morning, when Arznel flew far away over the woods, a stray, frightened bird flew across his path and in an instant, before their very eyes, the dragon caught it and ate it. Bella jumped up and down with excitement.

'He's become a hunter! Arznel will soon be able to hunt his own prey! The woods below are teeming with wildlife.'

Mia felt strangely uneasy as she watched the black dragon set off again, his eyes flashing mischievously.

Every afternoon, Bella insisted that Mia study with her in the library. The musty room was packed with shelf after shelf of mysterious books.

'You have much to learn, Mia child, and these books will help to feed your brain. Knowledge is a powerful magic in its own way!' she declared.

The Apothecary's Book of Herbs, *A History of Aland*, *Dragon Lore*, *The Geography of Arbor*, *A Beginner's Guide to Sorcery*, were just some of the many tomes that Bella expected Mia to read.

The old woman sat with Mia, explaining things or making her write down notes. The little girl tried to concentrate, all the time wishing that she was back in school with her friends.

She found a book on dragon anatomy and, looking at the detailed pictures, she began to wonder about Trig. Going by the diagrams and detailed sketches, Trig's wing and tail seemed healed, so why would Bella not let him fly?

At night, in the secrecy of her room, Mia held training sessions for the young dragon, letting him jump down from the bed and then, when he'd mastered that, progressing to the top of the wardrobe and the inside window ledge. There was very little space and she was always worried that he would injure himself again, or that Bella would discover them. She planned to take him out one morning to the courtyard, before the old woman woke, and let him try out his wings properly in the smallest training pen.

She was learning to be careful around Bella. Any mention of home or family or Glenkilty put the old woman into a ferocious temper.

'She promised me that I could go home!' she complained to Gwenda. 'Why won't she let me leave?'

But the dwelf girl simply kept on working, not wanting to tell her that she should forget about going home, forget that she ever had another home. Bella's apprentices were always homesick and miserable for the first year or two, until finally they forgot their families and homelands.

'The sad feeling will pass, Mia. In time you will forget,' she said.

Mia blinked away her tears. She would never forget her Mum and Dad, her brother Rory and Granny Rose, and her little dog, Jackie, no matter what Bella did or what spell she cast over her!

Chapter 20

The Map Room

Mia could scarcely believe it – Trig was able to fly! The blue dragon flew smoothly from the ground right up to the top perch, then swooped skywards, almost crashing into the net that prevented him escaping or falling out over the castle walls. She had never seen anything like it as he shimmered blue in the dawn. Their secret, early morning lessons had worked!

'Oh, Trig!' she laughed, hugging him tight. His eyes shone proudly as he nuzzled playfully against her cheek. Again and again the dragon flew, determined and excited. Mia wished that she could let him fly out into the open sky, but she knew it was too dangerous yet to risk that. They were both imprisoned by the whims of the Dragon Woman, unable to escape.

Trig had managed to learn to fly in secret, and she too was determined to find a way to escape from Bella and the castle. If only she knew where the old witch had hidden the feathered flying coat.

She remembered a story her Granny had often told her about a fisherman who had fallen in love with a Selkie and married her. Fearful of losing his bride, he had hidden his Selkie wife's sealskin so that she could never return to the sea. One day, after many long years, one of her children found the strange, rolled-up bundle of skin, and the Selkie wife put it on and joyously returned to the sea and her own Selkie folk. It was a good story. Mia decided that she would search the castle until she found the flying coat that would help her get back home where she belonged.

That morning, Bella had given Mia a list of cleaning jobs to help Gwenda with, as she had other matters to attend to. Grumbling, Mia carried a heavy bucket of water and a mop all the way up to the top of the enormous staircase.

'You can start with my bedroom!' Bella had ordered, and Mia couldn't help but wonder why she didn't just use some magic spell or other to make the room spick and span herself.

'Good, old-fashioned elbow grease is what is needed,' answered the old woman firmly, reading her thoughts.

Bella's room was in the large corner turret of the castle, with three enormous windows that looked out over the woods and the lake. A large, four-poster bed stood in the centre of the room, an embroidered coverlet of multicoloured dragons spread across it. The colours were faded now, but Mia searched for any blue ones that might resemble Trig. A washstand, similar to the one in her own room, stood in one corner, and on the opposite wall hung a stiff wall tapestry depicting a solitary green dragon who towered above a beautiful young girl. The dragon seeming to be listening to the flaxen-haired maiden. Between the wall and the bed lay a tower of books, some precariously balanced, some covered in dust. Getting out her cloth, Mia began to dust them. She glanced at the titles: *Sorcery of the Middle Ages*, *Potions and Portents*, *The New Alchemist*. Four or five books were strewn on the ground under the bed, forgotten most likely, and cleaning the dust off them she put them back on the stack. She was about to replace the very last one when she read the illuminated lettering on its side. *Olde Magick*, it read simply. It smelled of mould and its pages were stiff and yellow with age. Intrigued, Mia turned over the pages. This might be the very book she needed. Out of some strange instinct, she hid it in the deep pocket of her apron, and she continued cleaning.

'Mia, I'll finish up here,' offered Gwenda, appearing with fresh bed linen. 'You could perhaps start on the room at the end of the corridor.'

The door to the room was stiff when she opened it and the dust made her cough. Heavy, purple drapes covered the window and when she opened them a flood of light swept across the room, the dust spinning and hanging in the air. It was some kind of map room, every wall was covered with huge maps of places that lay outside the castle. Dark Wood, Giants' Valley, she read. Two maps contained pale sketches of mountains, showing the locations of towns and villages, and heavy gold paint traced out flying routes. Reading the cartographer's words, Mia realised that a vast world existed beyond the castle and its walls.

Perhaps the flying coat was hidden somewhere in this room, she reasoned. She began to search. Charts and heavy, leather-covered volumes filled the tall shelves that stretched to the high, wooden-beamed ceiling. What a collection! The dampness of the room had made spots of mould appear on the yellowing cloth and paper. The map room certainly needed attention.

A heavy, gold compass lay on a table in front of the window, and beside it one of the most beautiful things she had ever seen   a curved glass ball. A true craftsman had cut the glass with fine, intricate patterning, yet the ball was filled with a dirty-looking liquid. How did such a beautiful piece get to be used for stagnant old water, she wondered. Sunlight shimmered through the window, releasing from the sphere of glass a cascade of wildly coloured reflections, diamonds and stars and whorls of blue, green and yellow danced around the dull room. Before Mia's eyes, the water inside the bowl changed to a sparkling blue-green colour. Staring into it in astonishment, she could see her own face reflected, then the water became greener, a dash of blue appeared above, and a scene appeared in the glass globe that looked like a forest with the sky above it. How did it catch that reflection? She could see a flock of white birds flying across the tops of the trees, wings outstretched as they glided on the wind. Through the window, there was no sign of such a flock. Looking closely, she could make out two figures moving through the dense growth. One wore a bow slung across his shoulders, the other had his head down, concentrating on trying not to stumble. She leaned closer. They were unaware that she could see them.

'No!' A loud scream made her jump with fright. The old woman flew across the room. 'What are you doing, stupid girl?' Bella flew at her, pulling her hair. 'This room is forbidden to you. How did you get in here?'

'But I was going to clean it for you!' Mia didn't want to get Gwenda into trouble and said nothing else.

'Look at this light! Do you know what sunlight would do to these valuable charts and maps?' Bella shouted.

Mia shook her head miserably.

'It would turn them to dust.' Taking a pinch of dust, the old witch flung it in Mia's face.

'Did you touch anything, play with anything in this room?' she demanded.

'No!'

'Are you sure?' Bella looked around before pulling the drapes closed.

Mia nodded, and noticed that the glimmer of the crystal glass ball was extinguished. She tried to clear all thought of it from her head as Bella swung around to stare at her.

'Have you nothing to tell me?' she asked slyly. 'You have a guilty look on your face.'

Mia stared at the wooden floor, counting how many pieces

of timber the carpenter had used, hiding her thoughts from the sorceress.

Bella stared at her intently for a long time.

'I am sorry, child!' she said finally. 'I shouldn't have scared you so, it's just that no one is permitted in this room because of these fragile, ancient maps. Do you understand?'

Mia lifted the bucket and mop and cloth.

'Leave the cleaning, Mia. Go to your room and rest! You look tired, child.'

'Thank you!' said Mia softly, and she went back downstairs.

Returning to the map room, Bella touched her precious crystal ball and reopened the drapes to let the light catch the glass. She gazed angrily as the waters cleared and stilled. The boy and his companion had covered much ground, journeying further than she had anticipated. Creepers were stupid creatures! She would have to put fresh obstacles in their way. That boy must *never* reach his sister!

Chapter 21

The Wolves

Rory was glad of a companion on his journey. Conrad wasn't the talkative type, but Rory definitely felt safer having the young woodsman around. He was tired and fed up of the trees and the silence, and he could feel a large blister developing on his foot.

'Look, Rory!' whispered Conrad suddenly, pointing to a flock of large, white birds that flew almost over their heads. Pulling an arrow from his quiver, Conrad shot it high into the air, killing one of the birds.

'What is it?' asked Rory, who'd never seen a bird like it before.

''Tis a gullion. They taste very good roasted.'

Conrad set Rory the task of lighting the fire and providing all the kindling, while he plucked and cleaned the bird, a job Rory was glad not to do. The fire eventually flamed into life and Rory was glad to flop down and rest, taking off his shoes to let the air cool his feet. His socks were soaked with sweat and smelled awful, so he hung them out on a branch to dry.

Conrad speared the bird on a triangle of branches which he placed over the fire, then he skewered what looked like huge mushrooms, purple-coloured onions, and chunks of white turnip, turning them over and over again, like kebabs. Rory's mouth was watering by the time the food was cooked and he almost burnt his lips eating it.

'Mmmm, it tastes good!'

'An army marches on its stomach. That's what my father always used to say!' grinned Conrad, chewing on a meaty piece of leg-bone.

'I'm not sure that we're much of an army!'

'Well, that's no matter.'

'Where's your father now, Conrad?' Rory asked hesitantly.

'My father's dead, Rory. He died two winters ago when the high snows came. He went out hunting for boar but he disturbed one and it killed him! My Uncle Vern found him a month later, when the snows melted, frozen solid. He was a good man,' said Conrad, poking at the fire with a stick. 'My father taught me to hunt and fish and look after myself. My mother passed away when I was a small boy with a sickness we call River Fever, so my father raised me on his own. Now my uncle and aunt care for me. They're the only family I've got.'

Rory could see the pain and loneliness in the other boy's face. It must be awful to be so alone.

'Enough of my sad stories. Tell me about your family, Rory!'

'Well, there's just the two of us, Mia and me. Dad works in a bank and Mum has a part-time job in the local chemist's shop. We live in a place called Glenkilty. We share the house with my Granny Rose. It's near a small village where nothing much happens. We're just an ordinary family, very ordinary people!'

'You're lucky, Rory, to belong to such a family. I envy you.'

Rory reddened. He had never thought of his family like that at all.

Conrad tossed the bone away. 'But, what I can't understand is why Bella chose you and your family. What brought her to your village?'

Rory shrugged. 'Bella told Mia that she'd found an ancient dragon's nest in the woods near our house. Mia believed her. Mia told me she'd seen the young dragons with her own eyes. I thought Mia was just making the whole thing up. As well as that, she went and told the old woman that Dad is a magician.'

'A magician?'

'But he isn't! He works in a bank, looking after other peoples money, their accounts. That's his proper job. The magic is just a hobby. He's not even that good at it! Anyway, Mia told Mrs Blackwell all about him being an amateur magician, and then that barmy old woman kept on saying that Mia was a magician's daughter and she wanted her to become an apprentice dragon keeper, or some kind of nonsense like that.'

138

Conrad was staring at him with a wild, excited look in his eyes. 'A magician's daughter? Your sister is a magician's daughter!'

'No, Conrad, she's not! She's just ordinary!'

'Rory, you don't understand. Only a great magician or one of his kind has the ability to communicate with and understand dragons. They are the rarest and most intelligent – and most special – of creatures. He or she who controls the dragons has immense power. They say that the days of old magic will return when the dragons come back to the woods of Arbor. The sorceress has grown old and weak now, and she would need an apprentice, someone to learn the powers of deep magic before it's too late. That's why she has taken your sister! This is not ordinary, Rory. This is more special than you can imagine.'

Rory stared at the crackling wood on the fire. He didn't want to believe this old mumbo-jumbo about Mia. What did this stranger know, anyway!

'If Mia is a magician's daughter, Rory, you do realise what this means?' asked Conrad, leaning close to him.

'What?'

'That makes you a magician's son, my friend. You must be able to learn the old magic too!'

'Don't be stupid! I'm not a magician and never want to be one either!' Rory shouted, pushing Conrad away from him and jumping to his feet. He'd had more than enough of this kind of nonsense and stomped off under the trees to calm himself down. When he returned, Conrad lay fast asleep beside the embers of the fire, and Rory settled down across from him.

✧ ★ ✧

'Rory! Wake up!'

The dark woods were filled with the lonesome howl of an unseen animal. It hung in the silence like a mournful echo before another howl followed it, and then another.

'Wolves!' breathed Conrad.

Fear punched Rory's chest. *Wolves*. Their eerie howling sent chills down his spine. He had never heard a sound like it.

'We must be swift and silent or they will get us! Come on, move!'

Rory grabbed his backpack and pulled on his shoes. Conrad was already up and running.

Rory had never run so fast in all his life. His ribs and lungs ached painfully as he followed the other boy, racing helter-skelter through the dense undergrowth, briars and thorns tearing at his skin. The blood was pounding so loud in his ears that he could hear the thumping of what seemed like a hundred paws inside his own head.

'Climb!' ordered Conrad, who had stopped and grabbed hold of Rory. He pointed towards the thick base of an oak tree.

Rory scrambled frantically, searching for footholds or branches to grab on to. He kept falling back, but finally, with

Conrad pushing him up from beneath, he managed to grab a sturdy branch and swing himself up into the tree. He reached back to pull Conrad up, only to discover that his companion was gone. Seconds later, the first grey wolf appeared, crashing through the undergrowth, followed by the rest of the pack. Transfixed with fear, Rory watched as they circled the tree. He could see their green eyes and open jaws, as they panted and sniffed the ground below him. Then the lead wolf took a huge leap, snapping and snarling at the boy above him. Rory tried to move higher, terrified the wolf would reach him. His backpack tumbled to the ground. Yelping loudly, the wolves tossed it between them, ripping a part of it before losing interest and turning their attention back to Rory.

How long would they stay below him, waiting for him to fall? Rory didn't know what to do. If only Conrad were with him.

He felt exhausted and tense, watching the waiting wolves below. He forced himself to stay awake and alert, as the dreadful howling went on and on. Suddenly, he heard a crazed yelping and snapping below him, and the wolves began to snarl at each other in a frenzy. Peering down, Rory saw the enormous frame of another wolf which seemed to be attacking them. It had powerful legs and a large, almost square head.

The leader of the pack leapt at the stranger, biting and snarling. The fight went on for a long time, neither animal willing to give up. Teeth marks punctured their bodies as they yelped with pain. Then one cried harder and longer than the other, his coat matted with blood, before slinking away into the darkness of the wood. The rest of the wolves howled balefully at the moon, then retreated, leaving the winner standing alone. Rory gasped in disbelief – below him stood the Shadow Hound, he was sure of it! Once again the great hound had come to his rescue. He tried to climb down to it, but by the time he reached the ground the huge wolfhound had disappeared.

Chapter 22

Conrad

In desperation, Rory searched everywhere for Conrad. He prayed that his friend had not been attacked or injured by the ferocious wolves. But there was no sign of him anywhere.

Retrieving his backpack, which bore the marks of wolf fangs, Rory studied the crumpled map. He knew he had to resume his journey. He decided to head north, in the direction of the lake – from the map it seemed that there was a castle close by. Mia was there, he could sense it!

About midday the next day, Conrad appeared out of nowhere, startling him. He looked pale and wretched, his face cut and bruised and he moved slowly, as if he had torn a muscle.

'I thought the wolves had got you!' Rory breathed a sigh of relief. 'Where were you? I searched everywhere. I thought you were dead.'

Conrad pointed to a deep cut on the side of his head and a

purple bruise. 'I tried to get up in the tree after you, but when I saw the wolves' eyes coming closer and closer, I panicked kept running! I must have slipped and fallen because when I woke up, I'd rolled to the bottom of a river bank. By the time I got back you'd gone, so I tracked you.'

'Are you okay?'

'I'll live, don't worry!'

'By the way, thanks, Conrad.'

'That's okay, too!'

Over the next day or two they walked slowly, both of them tired, chatting along the way. Rory tried to explain the Internet and CD Rom to his bewildered companion. They nearly came to blows when Rory told him about his father's mobile phone and their television and video player.

'You're a liar!' jeered Conrad.

They were both incredulous at the amazing things in each other's worlds.

The terrain changed and they seemed to be climbing slightly. They had no bread or meat left, and their stomachs grumbled with constant hunger. They sat down to eat the last of their food, the large, dried-out oatcakes that the giants had given him. They were over-spiced for the boys' tastes, but they were glad enough of them.

Above them, the cawing of angry rooks filled the air and, looking up, the boys noticed large rookeries in the trees. They watched as hundreds of rooks covered the trees around them. Then, from afar, came the rustling of wings and a cloak of jet black crows swept towards the boys. Plump wood pigeons came next, cooing menacingly as they landed on the mossy earth beside them. Rory had never seen so many birds all together.

Conrad munched thoughtfully. 'Rory!' he said finally. 'I don't want you to be afraid, but I fear there are strong forces at work in these woods. I think those birds are getting ready to attack us.'

Rory looked up, scared.

'Now, don't move. It's not like the wolves. There's nowhere for us to take cover from them.'

Rory looked at his friend. What did he want him to do? Expect him to do? The birds reminded him of Bella, and he was convinced that she had sent them!

Neither the boys nor the birds moved at first, both aware of each other. Then, a screeching magpie launched the attack, flying into Conrad's face. More magpies followed, all swooping and diving at the boys, who threw their arms over their heads in an effort to protect themselves.

'Grab a stick!' gasped Conrad, as a swirling mass of black crows descended on them. Rory waved the narrow branch, and screamed loudly as he whacked it at the birds. He passed a branch to Conrad. Birds covered his friend's clothes and pecked at his black hair. The skin on Rory's arms was already torn and bleeding as he hit out uselessly at their enemies. Pulling an arrow from the leather holder, Rory plunged it into the birds that were attacking Conrad, jabbing at the mass of feathers and darting heads. But he knew that a few arrows and a bit of wood were not going to be enough to drive the birds away.

Conrad kicked and fought frantically, but the birds forced him on to the ground. Rory stabbed again and again as flapping pigeons pecked at his chest and throat. Conrad's body lay covered from top to toe with birds, fluttering and rustling all over him.

They're killing him, thought Rory, tears running down his face.

A sound of heavy, rushing wings filled the darkening sky above them. More birds, thought Rory. The crows and rooks and magpies and myriad other birds took no notice – they were too intent on attacking the boys. This time, enormous wings sent a gusting breeze towards them.

Rory looked up to see a large black and gold dragon! It was only a few feet from where they were. Seeming to ignore them, the powerful creature swung its heavy tail and body in the direction of the birds, sniffing the air excitedly. The rooks and crows took to the air, cawing furiously. The wood pigeons were too slow to move and the dragon scooped a lot of them into its mouth. The dragon turned its head and, opening its jaws, blew a scorching, flaming breath in the general direction of the rising birds. A cacophony of noise and sounds seared through the forest, a blackthorn tree burst into flames as the dragon resumed its flight. The terrified birds scattered in every direction.

'Where did that come from?' gasped Rory with relief.

Conrad lay totally still on the ground. Frightened, Rory rushed over to check him, rolling him on to his back. Conrad's eyes were closed, and he seemed to be in some kind of a deep trance. Bruises and scratches covered his arms and hands. His skin felt cold and clammy.

'Conrad, wake up! They're gone, the birds are gone!'

'So the enemy is vanquished,' murmured Conrad, beads of sweat clinging to his brow.

'Yeah! The birds are gone.'

'Let me rest, Rory. I'm drained from using so much energy. I need to rest.'

Immense relief coursed through Rory's veins and he began to shake with delayed shock. Imagine, a dragon had saved them! It was the most incredible thing he'd ever seen. He gave Conrad a few sips of water and poured the rest over his injured hands.

'I'm going to get us some more water, Conrad,' he said, 'so don't move till I get back.'

A few hundred yards away, he found a stream of icy cold water. Filling the two water flasks, he splashed the water on to his own bites and cuts.

It was when he stood up to turn back that he noticed it, the stone turret of a castle, peeping through a gap in the trees, less than a day's walk away.

'Conrad!' he shouted, running back. 'We're nearly there. I can see the castle!'

Chapter 23

The Candlemaker

At night, in the privacy of her room, Mia studied the *Olde Magick* book in secret. The writing was curved and looped, the language ancient and difficult to decipher, yet somehow Mia sensed it was important that she master some of the lessons it contained. It had been written for young wizards and witches, and contained lessons and spells about all sorts of things: how to turn a rusty pot copper again and make it shine; how to make a barking dog quiet; how to make a fish jump into a net; and deeper magic, like how to shape-change. For this it the book advised starting small, by changing oneself or someone else into a toad or a mouse or small kitten! Luckily it also gave instructions as to how to reverse the process.

One night Mia tried to change herself into a kitten, but succeeded only in developing a few whiskers and two pointy, black ears, before nervously reversing the spell. The spells to become invisible, or to change straw to gold, or rain to sunshine, were far too complicated.

✧ ✦ ✧

'Magnificent!' cried Bella, as Arznel looped so high in the sky that he appeared to touch the sun. Then, with a twist of his tail, he turned gracefully and landed noiselessly back beside the old woman in the middle of the courtyard. 'Well done!' she said, patting him. 'You are the finest of my dragons!'

Arznel tossed his head proudly. Mia leant forward and scratched him behind his ears. He always liked that. The other dragons jostled around her for attention too. Mia pulled out bacon rinds from her pocket, which she knew they loved.

'You have them spoiled, child, no wonder they adore you!' chided Bella gently.

The young dragons were all flying well. Oro was the most adventurous, showing off his air acrobatics. Even Dink, the clumsy one, had mastered the art of landing smoothly. Mia was proud of them all. But to her, Trig was still the finest of the dragons. His thoughts connected to hers. He was agile and quick, and by far the most intelligent. She couldn't wait for the day that Trig would fly with the others.

Bella had begun to let the dragons hunt, encouraging them to catch the odd bird or small animal that they spotted from the sky. The dragons thrived on the sport.

'I know you don't like it, Mia, but the dragons have to be

able to catch prey to survive. It's part of their training.'

'What'll happen to them when they're fully trained?' asked Mia. 'Will you release them into the woods?'

Bella shook her head. 'Many years ago, when I was a girl, the woods below were filled with dragons. But they were hunted down and killed. Armies of soldiers and knights were sent out from many kingdoms to rid the world of their dangerous presence. Dragons' teeth, scales and claws became valuable trophies for silly men to ride home with. They were smoked out from their caves and secret places, and the rivers ran red with dragons' blood as they were slaughtered. You see, humans were afraid of dragons, they could not understand them or recognise their beauty. Unfortunately, what humans do not understand, they destroy. No, the dragons are far safer here with me, child.'

'But what will happen to them?'

'They will grow big and learn to fight and defend themselves. In time they will breed and have young of their own, and you will watch them grow and learn, Mia. It's our job to ensure the survival of these precious dragons and the return of deep magic to the woods and fields of Arbor. You must realise by now, Mia, that the power of a true mage and dragon keeper entails great responsibility.'

Of late the old woman was often tired and took a nap or retired early in the evening. Mia grabbed every opportunity she could to search the castle in the hope of finding the flying coat, trying to imagine where the old sorceress might have hidden it. She realised that Bella had absolutely no intention of letting her return home. At night, in her room, she cried, Trig licking her tears away. Great waves of homesickness and loneliness washed over her as she thought of her mother and the family she would probably never see again.

✧ ✦ ✧

'The child is looking peaky, moping around the place!' Bella remarked. Take her to the village with you, Gwenda, but mind you don't let her out of your sight.'

'You can help me with the provisions,' offered Gwenda kindly, giving Mia a willow basket to carry. Mia couldn't mask her delight at having a few hours' break from the castle and the old woman.

''Tis a fair walk, Mia, but the day is fine and we have many errands,' smiled Gwenda, as they trudged along companionably over hilly countryside towards a place called Dwarf Vale.

'I grew up in these parts,' said Gwenda, her blue eyes sparkling with pride. 'There's Morgan's field – they say that the soil there is so rich and fertile that no matter what Farmer Morgan grows, it is twice the size and twice the flavour of anybody else's. Let's see what fresh produce he can sell us today.'

A neat, white farmhouse nestled close to a winding river surrounded by lush farmland spreading in all directions. Fields of cabbages and carrots and giant runner beans, and row after row of onions encircled the house. In a nearby field, a small, stout dwarf farmer was bent over at his work, a battered straw hat protecting his head from the sun's glare. Seeing them, he came over and began to walk them up and down between the abundant rows of his latest crops. Gwenda touched the plants, checking them carefully. Mia watched as the farmer lifted cabbage heads and bunches of carrots and placed them in Gwenda's basket, at the same time picking a seed from one of the many pockets in his smock coat and pushing it back into the very spot from which he had just lifted the plant.

Mia gazed in amazement – before her eyes a tiny, green shoot appeared instantly as a new plant began to grow!

'I will deliver the rest of the things you want to the castle tomorrow if that suits, Gwenda,' promised the farmer.

Bidding goodbye and thanks, Gwenda marched briskly on to the next farm. Hens and geese and ducks all scrabbled for their attention as they crossed the farmyard where pretty twin sisters were busy feeding the poultry.

'One hundred eggs of various types and sizes,' ordered Gwenda.

One hundred! Mia couldn't believe it. Her jaw dropped and her eyes opened wide with surprise.

'Are you fly-catching?' joked Gwenda. 'They're for the dragons, who are more than partial to eggs. Next is the rat farm.'

'Rat farm!'

Gwenda's plump face broke into a wide smile when she

saw the look of disgust and fear in Mia's eyes. ''Tis only another farm, my girl!'

Mia was terrified as they followed the curve of the road and saw the rusty gateway and the carved sign above it: Rowan-croft's Rat Farm. Beyond that was a ramshackle farm with a collection of broken-down outbuildings.

'This is my cousin's place,' declared Gwenda. 'It's gone to rack and ruin but he's hoping that business will improve now with the return of the dragons.'

Shivers ran down Mia's spine when she saw the seething mass of black and brown rats collected in low pits and fenced-in areas. They were squirming and wriggling and frantic, all trying to escape. She sat herself up on a stone post, well away from them.

'They're farmed rats, Mia. How many of those do you think it takes to feed a young dragon?' asked Gwenda, matter-of-factly.

Mia felt queasy even thinking about it and decided that this was one aspect of dragons that she'd prefer not to know about. She watched silently as Gwenda and her cousin discussed business.

Dwarf Vale itself was a collection of small dwellings and shops built into the shelter of a copse of low trees. Smoke curled from the chimneys and children ran about playing hide-and-seek. A group of stout dwarf women chatted together as they queued outside a provisions store. Gwenda and Mia joined them. Once inside the store, Gwenda bought flour, tea, butter, ginger and marmalade. The other customers all stared at Mia in curiosity. At the butchers, pork, two chickens and a joint of lamb were added to their baskets. Their final call was to the workshop of a candlemaker. Mia watched with fascination as Bernard Rathbone, an elf with a mop of grey hair, poured boiling-hot wax into long trays of narrow moulds, then trimmed the wicks. The heavy smell of tallow filled the air as the candlemaker read Gwenda's order and slipped it silently into his top pocket.

'Who is this strange little thing you have with you, Gwenda? She's not dwarf or elf, is she?'

'She's Bella's apprentice,' explained Gwenda.

'And how do you find the castle, young apprentice?'

Mia didn't know what to say. The candlemaker's eyes were brown, flecked with orange, and she felt like he could see right inside her soul.

'It's dark!' blurted out Mia.

The candlemaker threw back his head and laughed. Taking an armful of candles from a stand behind him, he filled her basket with them, layering them in sizes.

'Well, we can't have anyone afraid of the dark, now, can we?'

The candlemaker searched along one or two shelves and then called Mia over and handed her a small, cream coloured candle. She was about to put it in the basket with the rest of them when he grabbed hold of her wrist.

'This candle is for you, young apprentice!' he whispered.

'Keep it on you. You may have need of it someday.'

Curious, and slightly bewildered, Mia thanked him, hiding the candle in a roomy pocket in her skirt, the candlemaker's long, narrow face remaining expressionless as he began to melt another batch of foul-smelling animal grease and fat to make more candles.

All the way back to the castle, Mia wondered about what the candlemaker had said: what could it mean?

Chapter 24

The Crystal Ball

During the night Mia returned to the map room, anxious to search it one more time. Bella had been so insistent that she should never again go in there, she believed that the room must hold some important secret!

The door was locked. She tried with all her might to open it. It wouldn't budge. Not willing to give up, she decided to try one of the tricks she had learned from the *Olde Magick* book. She pulled a clip from her hair, and holding it in her hand stared hard at it. She must use the power of her thoughts to convince the old metal hair-clip that it was a key, the exact key for this lock, the key that would open this door and let her in.

Not relaxing her mind for a single second, she felt the clip grow heavy, its shape slowly changing as it became the key of the map room door. She put the key in the lock and almost whooped for joy when the door swung open before her.

It took her only a few minutes of rooting around to discover that the map room did not contain the flying coat. Disappointed, she looked around her, and was drawn once again to the glass ball on the table.

By the faint glow of candlelight, the glass looked dull and insignificant, nothing special at all. Maybe if she opened the drapes slightly? A crescent moon peeped in through the gap in the heavy, damask cloth. The glass ball slowly turned a pale cream colour. As Mia lifted it up to look at it, the liquid inside turned milky. All she could see in it was her own face, her large eyes and nervous mouth and loose, tumbling hair. She sighed with vexation and disappointment. The ball wasn't magic at all!

She thought of home, a picture instantly filling her mind. The ball became warm in her hands, she could feel the liquid inside it moving. She almost dropped it with shock on seeing her house appear in its glassy curves. It was raining lightly and she could see the raindrops running down the window of her own bedroom. But the house looked dark and empty! Thoughts of the house next door, came, unbidden, into her mind and she was shocked to see Bella's old house, covered in a rampant green and yellow ivy that almost covered the front of the house. Roses had appeared around the windows and doors, pink dusky blooms heavy with rain, while a huge daisy bush almost blocked the path to the porch.

What was the ball telling her? she wondered. In a panic she thought of her Mum and Dad. Please let me see them, she wished. The colour of the glass began to change, becoming almost clear as her mother's puzzled face appeared. Mia could see her so clearly, the freckles on her forehead, the way she wrinkled her nose when she concentrated on something. She was sitting at a dining table, surrounded by people. The man next to her was trying to talk to her, but Mum was ignoring him. She looked up from the table, turning her head this way and that and then looked straight ahead, worried, frowning, before resuming conversation.

'Mum, it's me!' sobbed Mia, as she watched her mother turn and make polite dinner conversation. Her Dad sat across from her. Matthew Murphy suddenly sat bolt upright as if seeing her, his eyes staring straight ahead of him. Mia concentrated on her Dad. 'Mia' – she could read his lips saying the word. Then the ball changed again, becoming a swirling mass of colours, the images disappearing. She took a deep breath – what about Rory and Granny Rose? The ball was useless, no help at all, showing her some kind of woods, the trees too thick for her to see anything in the darkness, and then just a rose. Annoyed, she put the glass ball back down, watching the liquid inside settle.

At least she had seen her parents, but as they seemed to be still in America, they must be unaware of her disappearance.

Mia felt utterly lost and alone. Without the flying coat, she would never be able to find her way home again, and in time her family would forget about her and get on with their own lives. She would spend the rest of her life imprisoned here in the castle with Bella, training to be an apprentice mage or wizard, or whatever the old woman wanted her to become, her only consolation the dragons whom she cared for.

Making sure the room looked untouched, she closed the drapes and locked the door behind her, slipping silently down the stairs and back to her room, where Trig waited patiently. The blue dragon nuzzled her with his snout and licked her with his rough, scratchy tongue.

'Oh, Trig! What am I going to do?' sighed Mia. 'I just want to go back home!'

Chapter 25

Enchanted

The morning air was deliciously cool and crisp. The other dragons were still sleeping as Trig and Mia crossed the courtyard. The blue dragon looked towards the sky wistfully as Mia led him to the training pen. Suddenly, she stopped and, guessing what he was thinking, she led him towards the open courtyard.

'You want to fly free like the rest of them, Trig, don't you? Well, now's your chance!'

Trig stood obediently, his legs planted firmly on the ground, his thick, curving tail lashing back and forth with excitement as the stiff, spiked scales along his back stood erect. His wings began to flap. Mia patted his neck. His ears were raised in attention and his eyes eager.

'You can do it, Trig! You can fly just as well as the others. 'Off you go!' she ordered.

The dragon took a few quick running steps, then lifted off

into the great, wide, blue above.

'Fly!' She shouted as she ran along the ground beneath him.

The young dragon's nervousness disappeared as he flew higher and higher. The sun's rays caught his scales, the light making them sparkle like a sapphire, his wings and tail and head touched with glistening gold. Mia had never seen anything so perfect as Trig, *her* dragon. She gazed at the beautiful creature as he flew out over the castle and across the lake and surrounding countryside. Her eyes shone with pride.

For half an hour she watched him, so engrossed that she didn't hear Bella's footsteps as she came up the stairs and across the stones.

'So this is the work of my apprentice! The treachery! I've been betrayed by a trusted child!'

Mia's heart froze. She turned around to see Bella, still in her night-dress, her hair streaming from her head like a banshee.

'Why, Mia? Why did you deceive me?' asked the old woman angrily. 'Have I not been kind to you, looked after you?'

Mia nodded miserably as Trig circled above her.

'I have a mind to turn you into a mouse or a rat and feed you to your precious dragon,' threatened the sorceress.

'I just wanted to surprise you, Bella, show you that Trig can fly,' Mia tried to explain. 'His injuries have healed and I've been working with him and training him for the past few days. Just look at him! He's the most beautiful dragon ever!'

But Bella's cheeks were flushed with temper. 'You disobeyed me! I was willing to share my secrets with you, and you dared to defy *me*, an all-powerful mage! This is how my kindness is rewarded, with lies and deceit. I will not tolerate it, Mia! As for the blue, you have practically made him untrainable.'

Mia didn't know what to do or say, or why Bella was so angry with her.

'You were the one who lied to me!' she said finally. 'You promised you'd let me return home once I'd helped you with the dragons. You promised me!' Mia stood in the centre of the courtyard, a small, determined figure, speaking her mind, her hair blowing in the breeze, her eyes serious. The blue dragon landed softly behind her.

'I want to go home!' she said defiantly.

'Home! What is home and family compared to the powers of magic and sorcery? To the wonders of being a dragon keeper? The woods below, Arbor, even perhaps, the kingdom itself could be yours in time, Mia child. Trust me!'

'I don't trust you. You're a liar! All I want is to go home and see my family. You promised me, Bella, you promised me!' Tears filled Mia's eyes and she blinked them away, not wanting to give the old woman the satisfaction of seeing her cry.

Bella stood in the morning light, confronted by the truth of Mia's feelings.

'Come here to me, child!' ordered the old woman softly, her voice coaxing.

Mia stood uncertain.

'Come, child! Come!'

Mia walked forward, trembling.

'These things are causing you pain. I will not have my favourite child upset so!'

'I want to go home! Please, Bella, let me go home!' Mia begged, almost hysterical.

'Hush, child! We will speak no more of it!' The old woman put her arm around Mia and held her close. Then she tilted the child's face upwards and Mia felt compelled look into the depths of those ancient eyes, unable to break the spell.

'All words and pictures of the past and the world you've left behind are banished from your troubled mind,' intoned Bella. 'There will be no more tears or upsets, my young apprentice, for there is much work to be done.'

Frantic, Mia realised what Bella was doing and desperately tried to put her secret thoughts in a sealed box locked away in the most hidden part of her mind. But, like wool unravelling, memories and images of everything and everyone she cared about began to disappear. Mia could feel herself slipping away, the grey stones beneath her rushed to meet her as she fell to the ground.

'Mia! Are you all right?'

Mia sat up groggily. Gwenda was kneeling beside her, helping her up.

'Is the child all right?' she said. 'She must have fainted. Poor little thing, out here so early in the morning with Trig.

Take her inside, Gwenda and give her a big bowl of your hot porridge and honey.'

Mia stood up. Trig leaned forward, sniffing at her worriedly. She could see great love for her in his eyes. The old woman was staring at her intently as Mia rubbed her aching head and eyes. She felt strangely tired. What had happened? She remembered the old woman coming out to the courtyard, discovering herself and Trig, but nothing more after that. Feeling rather dizzy she followed Gwenda to the kitchen. The dwelf girl was unusually quiet as she served breakfast.

Mia stared into space, trying to figure out why she suddenly felt so different and afraid, as she ate spoonfuls of the hot, steaming porridge.

Chapter 26

The Silver Lake

The Silver Lake stretched out before them. A shimmering pool of silvery blue sparkling water, which rippled in the breeze, surrounded by shady trees. Across on the far side of the lake stood a grey, stone castle, its tall towers and turrets reflected in the water. This was the castle of the sorceress, the place where Bella had taken his sister and imprisoned her, Rory was sure of it.

He and Conrad walked along the shoreline, trudging through tall bulrushes and reeds that stood at the water's edge. The lake formed a natural moat around the castle. There was no sign of a bridge of any kind.

'We could swim!' suggested Rory.

'It's deep, far too deep,' admitted Conrad, 'and likely there's currents and water weed to contend with.'

For an hour they scouted around the lake, searching for some means of crossing that vast tract of water. It was Conrad who spotted a small punt approaching, the occupants rowing busily. The two boys hid in the tall reeds as the boat came closer. It was a dwarf father and son returning from a fishing expedition. They tied up their boat, and then lifted out their catch and fishing tackle before setting off home.

When the boys were sure the dwarves would not return, they ran down to the narrow, wooden jetty where the tiny boat was moored, waves lapping gently against it.

'Do you think it will hold both of us?' asked Rory.

It was a small craft, but Conrad reckoned that they could both just about squeeze into it.

'I feel like we're stealing it,' sighed Rory.

'We're not! We're just borrowing it!'

Rory wasn't so sure, but there was no other way to get across. Slipping the mooring rope, the two of them clambered in, the small boat, which was rocking giddily as they began to row. They sat one behind the other, each taking one of the short oars, the boat low in the water with their combined weight. The lake was choppy and they both had to pull at the oars to get the boat to move, trying to avoid strong currents near the centre of the lake.

'Look at the fish!' Rory had never seen anything like it.

All around them, the water turned to silver as fish swam around the boat, the water splashing wildly, the glinting shapes appearing and disappearing. Conrad stopped rowing He had never seen fish like this before. You could almost put your hand down and catch one, they were so plentiful.

Rory leaned over the side of the boat, trying to get a closer look, perhaps even to touch one. They were quick, swimming in formation, like silver ribbons weaving and darting back and forth.

'They're huge, Conrad, absolutely huge. They're almost the length of the boat.'

He had hardly said the words when the first silver eel tried to throw itself onto the small boat.

'They're eels!' started Conrad 'Silver eels! We've got to stop them, Rory, or they'll capsize us!'

As if by some unseen command the small craft came under siege from all sides as hundreds of winding, giant, wormlike eels flung themselves into the boat, destabilising it. Water poured in over the sides and filled up the bottom.

'Get them off! Using their oars, the boys tried to batter them back, pushing them down into the water only to see them return instantly on the attack again.

'You try and row, Rory,' yelled Conrad, 'and I'll try and get rid of them!'

The eels kept coming, a fierce, fixed gaze in their fishy eyes. Conrad hit and kicked them and, getting braver, caught them and flung them high in the air. But a few seconds later another wave of eels would appear.

Rory rowed as hard as he could, but the boat was weighted down by the hundreds of squirming eels that latched on to its sides and by the water that sloshed around their feet as the little boat began to flood. Conrad took a small blade from his side pocket and began to nick the skin of every eel that managed to get over the side. Shocked, it would wriggle back down to the watery depths, hopefully never to reappear. The boys battled on for hours, scarcely moving, until the eel attack began to ease. Then, Conrad started to row again, the silver eels moving with them as they pulled through the current. Putting their backs into it, the boys rowed in a strong rhythm, heading for a rocky promontory beneath the castle walls, hoping that the water would become too shallow for the eels to follow them.

Finally, they ran the small boat aground. The waters of the lake turned to a burning crimson as the sun began slowly to sink in the sky. The exhausted boys had reached the weed-covered rocks, under the shadow of Blackwell Castle.

Chapter 27

Within the Walls

'Stay down! Keep hidden or the sorceress will see us!' cautioned Conrad, hiding the boat in some tall, waving reeds. They moved silently along the base of the castle walls, looking for an entrance or gap that they could squeeze through. The walls were at least three feet thick and towered high above them.

A jet-black crow circling overhead spotted them and began a raucous cawing. Conrad stopped and swiftly drew an arrow from his quiver. Stringing it across his bow, he took careful aim as the bird flew overhead. The arrow sliced through the air and the crow tumbled from the sky, straight into the whirling waters of the lake below. As they watched the crow's body splash into the lake, they noticed that a section of the lake next to the walls was polluted by filthy, stagnant water.

'I wonder where that water came from,' said Conrad.

They both peered over the edge of the bank into it. Conrad

stretched out his hand and plunged it into the water.

'Look, Rory, there's a small opening here. We could get through it, I think! It must be an overflow water outlet. Come on! We'll fit.'

Not knowing what lay on the other side, they waded into the water, pushing their way through weeds and slime, their mouths shut tightly. The filthy ooze and stagnant water staining their clothes was disgusting and made them smell like a sewer. If Bella didn't see them coming, she'd surely smell them!

They emerged into some kind of huge, stone trough that was in sore need of cleaning, then stepped out into a courtyard, part of which was fenced off.

'Those are the dragon pens,' warned Conrad.

Rory was petrified. What if a dragon saw them?

They noticed a group of dragons in the distance, busy preening themselves and licking their skin, which shone in myriad colours against the grey stone. Rory was rooted to the spot in fear and awe. Everything his sister had told him about these magnificent creatures had been true!

Hiding behind a low stone parapet, they waited and waited. Eventually, a stocky girl appeared and went from pen to pen, leaving food on the ground for the young dragons to eat. Squeals of delight filled the air.

'Let's follow her,' urged Conrad.

The girl walked briskly through a narrow, arched doorway, down a stairwell and into a long corridor.

Silently they crept after her, then hid behind barrels and crates when she entered a room. It was the castle's kitchen. The dwelf girl began to prepare dinner and soon a delicious smell filled the air and the boys' empty stomachs groaned with hunger.

A clatter of footsteps moved along the stone floor. Rory gasped when he saw Mia approaching, accompanied by the bird woman! Mia wore a strange outfit, but no chains or ropes bound her. He watched in disbelief as she emptied a pot of green beans into a deep dish and carried it to the table. He wanted to rush out and grab her, tell her he was here and that she was safe now, but Conrad restrained him.

Bella sat at the top of the table. She wore a gown of peacock blue and her white hair was plaited and hung down her back. Mia sat close by her, passing her food and pouring water from a jug into the old woman's goblet. The dwelf girl sat down too and passed the plates around.

'We should jump out and snatch her! Do something!' Rory pleaded.

At that, Bella rose from her chair, sniffing the air like a dog. Her eyes searched the room, then narrowed.

'I do believe that we have visitors among us,' she announced sarcastically, 'or should I say *intruders*!'

The skin gleamed pale over the old woman's bony features, her eyes were black as beetles and the dragon-wing marks on her forehead taut as she called to them: 'Please, gentlemen! Come and join us! You are discovered!' She laughed wickedly, beckoning them.

Reluctantly, the two boys stepped forward from their hiding place.

'Mia!' shouted Rory, running to the table and hugging his sister. She drew back, alarmed. 'It's me! It's me Rory!'

A look of total bewilderment and confusion passed over his sister's face as she struggled to release herself from his embrace.

'Let go of me, stranger!' she begged.

'Mia!' he shouted, shaking her. 'Mia! You know who I am. It's me, Rory.'

It was as if Mia didn't know him at all, or couldn't understand the language he spoke. She looked embarrassed. What had happened to her?

'What have you done with the girl?' demanded Conrad, standing in front of the sorceress.

The old woman smirked. 'You may join us if you wish, for you both look half-starved. Eat and enjoy, for tomorrow who knows what pleasure I may have in store for you!'

In despair, they sat down at the table, all the fight and spirit gone out of them. Rory knew that their brave quest had been in vain. The old woman must have enchanted Mia with a spell. She didn't even recognise or remember him! Conrad had started to eat, but Rory just stared at the food, miserable. Now both of them were prisoners of the sorceress too. It couldn't end like this, he wouldn't let it. Mia *must* remember! He'd make her remember! He began to talk, his words filling the silence, and Bella looked bemused. He talked of their mother and father, the fun times they had growing up together in Glenkilty: birthday parties, Christmas, her first Holy Communion, Granny Rose, Jackie. The old witch began to get irritated as he told stories of Glenkilty and the people in the village and their school. Mia smiled, but he could see she remained untouched, uninterested in what he was saying.

'Sing!' whispered Conrad suddenly.

Rory felt stupid, but he tried to think of a song that Mia liked – or used to like. He racked his brains trying to remember songs they had sung back home, sitting round the table.

'Happy birthday to you, happy birthday to you, happy birthday, dear Mia, happy birthday to you.'

Only Gwenda, the dwelf girl, smiled at the strange song.

'Jingle bells, jingle bells, jingle all the way!' Rory sang frantically.

But his efforts were useless. It was all absolutely hopeless. Never again would he sit round a table with Mia and his Mum and Dad, arguing, his parents giving out to him about his manners ... he looked up, Mia was eating some kind of mashed up vegetable, lost in a trance, as if she was in a world of her own. From deep within, he drew a rumbling sound, letting it fill his belly, push up through his chest and slide up his throat. It was one of the biggest belches he had ever done!

A look of deep disgust and dismay flitted across Bella's face.

Mia's eyes opened wide. 'Rory!'

Almost knocking over the table, he rushed over to his sister, pulling her to her feet. 'You remember!'

She nodded, too terrified to laugh or smile.

'Run!' Conrad's words sent them racing out of the room and along the narrow corridor. The old witch screeched as she got to her feet. Rory had no idea where to go or in what direction, but he kept a tight hold of Mia's hand, frightened to lose her again.

'Keep on running and don't stop!' ordered Conrad.

They ran up and down passageways and corridors, as Bella, feet lifting off the ground, began to fly after them.

Mia led the boys, helter skelter, through the castle.

'In here!' she said, pushing them into the old banqueting hall.

'How will we get out of here?' panted Rory. 'What are we going to do?'

They all tried to get their breath back and think of some kind of plan.

'Rory, I'll try to lead Bella to the other end of the castle so you two can escape.'

'No, Conrad. You've done so much already. I'd never have found Mia without you.'

'Listen, Rory, I'm well able to look after myself and that ancient old sorceress doesn't bother me. Give me your red sweatshirt!'

Reluctantly, Rory pulled his hooded sweatshirt over his head and passed it to the other boy, who slipped it on.

'Make for the boat,' ordered Conrad, 'You know where it is. Wait a while for me, but not more than thirty minutes.'

'I'm not leaving without you!' promised Rory.

'Go!' said Conrad firmly.

They could hear Bella moving along the corridor, screeching, doors banging open and shut as she searched for them.

'She'll find us!' gasped Mia.

'Ssshh!' ordered Conrad. 'Give me a minute, then move!'

Rory and Mia watched in dismay as Conrad opened the door and began to run. A minute later they took off in the opposite direction.

Chapter 28

The Runaways

Mia and Rory stayed close together, determined not to be separated again.

'We must get to the stairs!' urged Mia.

Racing as fast as they could along the corridor, they prayed silently that Conrad had managed to outwit the devious Bella, too.

'Do you hear that?' gasped Mia, holding Rory's arm.

The air was filled with the sounds of yelping and barking as a frenzied pack of wild dogs set about hunting their prey. The witch must have summoned them, and already they were on Conrad's scent.

'Rory! We can't go downstairs, they'll attack us! What'll we do?'

'Back the way we came!' he shouted, knowing that Bella was gaining on them.

They passed the map room and Mia was tempted to hide there.

'Come on!' urged Rory. 'Conrad can only hold them off for so long, there must be another way to get down to the kitchen.

'There's a back stairs, but I've never used it,' said Mia, leading the way.

The door was stiff and they had to force it open. A musty smell assaulted them as they negotiated the narrow, winding, stone steps. There was no rail, and twice Mia nearly fell. They both stopped, frozen with fear, when they heard the door open above them. They hurled themselves down the rest of the way.

'Bella's there,' whispered Mia. 'She's waiting for us!'

'Is there another floor beneath this?'

'Just the dungeons,' Mia shrugged.

Rory urged his sister on into the darkness, and they crept deeper below into the depths of the castle.

Water dripped from the walls and it was freezing cold. It was so dark they could scarcely see a thing. Mia jumped as something brushed against her face.

'Just cobwebs, Mia!' Rory lashed at the space above and around him   Mia was afraid of spiders.

'It's okay,' said Mia. 'Our eyes will get used to the dark in a moment.'

Rory couldn't believe it, his little sister was unafraid of the dark, and trying to comfort *him*!

They both stayed perfectly still, holding their breath as Bella called them from somewhere in the castle.

'Give yourselves up, children! You know I'll find you,

wherever you are! You will never leave this castle!'

'I wonder if there is any way out of these dungeons and cells other than the way we came?' sighed Rory. 'Others must have escaped!'

Clasping her brother's hand, Mia followed him.

'If only we'd a candle or a torch or something,' he muttered.

'We do have a candle,' she remembered, retrieving from her pocket the small cream-coloured candle that the candle-maker had given her. 'If only it would light!'

The words had scarcely left her mouth when the wick flickered into flame.

The candle sent soft light shadows around the dungeon and its cells, illuminating the black walls and mouldy floors. Holding the candle up, Mia could see a thick layer of spider webs hanging from the ceiling. The black, beady eyes of the spiders watched them from the darkness. She closed her eyes. She'd always been afraid of spiders and now she longed to cry out to Bella to come and rescue her.

'It's all right, Mia!' assured Rory, wrapping her in his arms. 'They won't touch you. They're more frightened of us!'

Mia could see a huge, black spider looking down on them from its vantage point on the ceiling. The spider crept from its hiding place and dangled down on a fine, gossamer thread beside them. Then it dropped to the ground, ran along the wall and slipped out through a crack in the stonework. The same thought struck both children at once: the stones were moveable! They tugged at them and loosened them, eventually revealing a gap big enough for them to slip through.

'It must be a secret passageway,' said Mia. 'Come on!'

The passageway was steep and dark and damp, but the candle cast a comforting glow in the desperate darkness.

They soon realised the extent of the spider's help: all along the treacherous, slippy passageway the spider had left a trail of her finest webs. Following them, they soon felt the welcome breeze of fresh air and found themselves back outside the castle, near the rocky beach where the little boat lay hidden.

There they waited for Conrad to appear.

Eventually, they could wait no more. There was no sign of the other boy. Rory pushed the small boat out onto the lake. Deep in his heart he knew that the three of them would never have fitted in the dwarves' small fishing craft, and wondered if that was why Conrad had left them. The water was still and clear, with no sign of the attacking eels.

'Row!' he told Mia, as they pulled away from the shore, leaving the witch's castle behind. He should have been overjoyed at rescuing his sister, but all he could think of was what Bella would do to Conrad when she caught him.

'What's wrong, Rory?'

How could he begin to explain the bond that had developed between him and the young woodsman that had saved his life?

Mia rowed, the little craft ferrying them across the lake, each stroke taking them further and further away from Bella, the dragons and the castle. They had barely reached the safety of the shore when Mia spotted a black shadow darkening the sky.

'It's Arznel!' whispered Mia, dragging Rory under cover. 'He's searching for us!'

She knew Arznel must be scared, flying on his own as all trace of daylight began to leave the sky. He was probably so busy concentrating on landmarks that he was unable to scout the area well.

'Will Bella herself come after us, do you think?' asked Rory fearfully.

Mia wasn't sure. Who could say what lengths Bella would go to, or what she was capable of?

Once Arznel was out of sight, they quickly tied up the boat.

'We have to hide!' urged Rory. 'Deep inside the wood is safest – the dragons will find it harder to hunt us there.'

Chapter 29

Crosswinds

Darkness had fallen and Mia was scared. Each tree took on a haunting shape, curving and twisting like gnarled arms trying to catch her. Shadows moved and stretched everywhere and she was terrified that Bella would appear out of nowhere and grab her.

'Let's sit down, Mia, we should rest!' suggested Rory.

Mia set her candle to light. Its tiny, flickering flame burned brightly, and they both drew up close to it for the small comfort it offered. Mia still couldn't believe that her brother had been brave enough to follow her and find her. She began her story at the beginning, telling him all that had happened to her since that first night she had gone with Bella.

'It's all right, Mia, you're here with me,' he tried to reassure her. 'You're safe now!'

His sister seemed lost in her own thoughts, a troubled expression on her pretty face.

'I'll miss the dragons, Rory! I love them. Oh, Rory, did you see them? They're all so clever and bright, the most wonderful, intelligent creatures ever. I don't know how poor Bella will manage them, even with Gwenda helping. It'll be too much for her.'

Rory couldn't believe it! Mia was talking about the dragons and that castle and that horrible old witch as if they mattered to her, as if she *cared* for them!

'Are you mad, Mia? Did that witch take your brain? I nearly got killed trying to rescue you, a creeper nearly bit my fingers off, and Conrad ...' his breath came in deep shudders, 'he could be dead for all we know! Mia, you just don't know the half of it!'

'Then tell me!'

Rory told her of how he'd searched for her and of the great Shadow Hound that he had ridden through the night, and of Nilo and Birch and all the rest of the giants. He told her about the dangers and terrors he had experienced on his quest to rescue her, and of his good friend, Conrad, who had now sacrificed his own life to ensure their escape.

His sister's face was ghastly pale by the time he'd finished.

'I'm sorry, Rory!' she said softly. 'I don't know what would have happened if you hadn't come after me, and I'm really sorry about Conrad.'

Rory could see that his sister was close to tears.

'It's all right, Mia, we'll be home soon. Everything will be fine again, once we get back to Mum and Dad and Glenkilty.'

He tried to convince himself that everything would soon be back to normal.

'*How* are we going to get back?' asked Mia.

Rory gazed at the candle. He hadn't a clue how they were going to return to their own world. If only Conrad was with them, he'd know what to do.

'Listen, we'll talk about it in the morning. We're both tired and should get some sleep.'

In the morning, Rory unfurled the map from his battered backpack and spread it on the forest floor. He and Mia studied it as they shared the last, stale oatcake. He pointed out places he'd already been to.

'The Shadow Hound left me somewhere near there, and that's where Giants' Caves is. There's swampland there, and here's where I entered Dragon Wood.

Mia looked closely at the map, thinking of Bella's big maps with all the flying routes marked out. Closing her eyes, she tried to remember them.

'There should be a cross-roads somewhere around there,' she said, pointing at the map. 'All the flying routes cross through it, as if it's someplace important.'

Rory knelt on the ground, peering over the criss-cross patterns, the curved writing and arrows, the coloured-in markings of forest and river, lake and mountain. But still he could not see what Mia was pointing to.

'Look! There, Rory! You can see it.'

Suddenly he could see it – on the map a faint, yellow four-sided cross, pointing in four directions, like the centre of a compass, was marked.

'It's between the four territories, but it could be miles away, Mia. Will we be able to manage it?'

His sister nodded, already standing up, ready to go.

They left the woods and forests of Arbor behind. A carved, wooden signpost on the deserted, winding path pointed them in the direction of a place called Crosswinds. They journeyed on and on, too terrified to stop.

At Crosswinds, an enormous rocky mountain jutted up from the ground. It was so high, they couldn't even see the top.

'Well, this is it, the place marked on the map! What'll we do now?'

They walked around the base of the mountain. From the ground, looking up, it was the strangest thing – the jagged rocks took on the features of four huge, stone faces, each looking in a different direction: north, south, east and west.

'It must be some kind of ancient monument,' said Rory.

'I wonder what they are staring at? What are they waiting for?' asked Mia.

'Perhaps we should climb it, and see where it goes!' suggested Rory. 'There seems to be a sort of path.'

Mountain goats had worn a pathway upwards, over stone chippings and spiky grass, and the children stuck to it closely.

They arrived at the top, breathless and excited. Montan, Arbor, Terra and Mare, the four territories that made up the kingdom of Aland, were spread out beneath them.

Mia shivered. It was cold so high up, and the ground was covered with frost. The wind blew sharply around them.

'I think we should stay here,' suggested Rory. 'Maybe there's some way of getting back home from here!'

The wind grew stronger around them, blowing down from the mountains, chilling their bones. Rory wondered what Conrad would have done in this situation. The wind blew stronger and stronger, forcing itself through the crevices and cracks of the carved stone until it seemed that the ancient figures were moaning, trying to tell them something.

'Listen, Rory! Listen!' shouted Mia. 'Can you hear it! They're talking to us.'

Rory tried to make sense of the gusting, whistling sounds all about them.

Mia listened intently. '"Tomorrow!" they said. "Tomorrow when the west wind blows!"' she said excitedly, gripping his hand.

Rory nodded, he had understood the word 'west', but little else.

From their vantage point they spotted three dragons flying southwards, searching for them, a blaze of bright colour against the sky. Hunkering down, they hid in the shadow of the towering figures. They'd have to stay here until the next day – they didn't dare move for fear of attracting the dragons' attention.

Chapter 30

On Dragons' Wings

Mia's mind was in turmoil. Naturally, she longed to return home to her mother and father and Granny and Jackie, and to go back to school and see all her friends again. But she didn't know how she could bear to be without her young dragons, not to have Trig snuffle his snout against her hand, nor ever again to listen as Bella explained magical tricks to her. This strange, secret land had become a part of her, and she wasn't sure if she was ready to leave it. For Rory, everything was always simple and uncomplicated, but for her it was different. Magic and keeping dragons had become second nature to her, and she really wasn't sure she wanted to give them up.

The temperature had dropped further during the night, and they were both freezing cold and wishing they had a warm jacket or blanket. Rory had refused to light a fire, fearing it would give away their position to the vigilant dragons, so they huddled against the rocks for protection.

The morning brought the welcome heat of the sun, and a magnificent view spread out below them. The wind was increasing, catching Mia's hair, tossing it around, making it hard for her to catch her breath.

'Look!' whispered Rory.

They both stared as, in the distance, two dragons, wings stretched wide, flew across the sky, the sunlight burnishing them silver and gold. Perhaps this would be the last dragon flight either of them would ever see. They watched the two dragons as, buffeted by the wind, they flew together in perfect harmony, a magnificent black ... and a blue.

'Rory, it's Arznel and Trig!'

'Hide!' shouted her brother, for already the dragons were turning and flying back in the direction of Crosswinds.

Fascinated, Mia watched as the two young dragons flew towards them. Rory pushed her onto the ground, where thick bracken and tumbling heather covered the rocks.

The dragons circled and circled above them, calling to each other, their eyes glittering as they searched the undergrowth from on high. Then they began to descend, flying lower and lower, wings folding, until finally they thudded gently to earth.

Mia could feel her heart thumping in her ribcage. Trig would surely hear it too. He had lifted his head and was sniffing, his snout quivering. Even in the raging wind he could smell her. Trig knew she was here.

Mia peeped out at the dragon she cared for so much. Arznel stood behind Trig, his tail and wings rippling in the air. She wasn't afraid, Trig wouldn't harm her. She started to get up, but Rory flung himself at her, wrestling her onto the ground.

'No, Mia!' he pleaded, trying to keep hold of her wrist and waist. 'Don't be crazy!'

'Let me go, Rory!' she said, pushing him off. 'The dragons will not harm us.'

Rory watched, mesmerised, as his sister got up and walked calmly over to the two dragons. She petted the big black one and wrapped her arms around the smaller blue one, hugging him affectionately.

She noticed that a small leather pouch had been fastened around Trig's neck. She removed it and opened it up. Inside, there was a crumpled pieces of paper. As she read it, she began to look troubled. Mia stood there, forlorn, the piece of paper in her hands.

Rory dashed forward, forgetting his fear of the dragons as Mia passed the short message to him.

Bella is dying. You must return to Blackwell Castle. You are needed urgently. The dragons will take you. Signed, A Good Friend.

The two of them read and reread the message, trying to make sense of it. Perhaps it was the old witch's final trick? Or had Gwenda sent it? Could Conrad still possibly be in the castle?

'It's a trick!' insisted Rory. 'The witch is just trying to get you back! Don't believe her!'

'I'm going back,' declared Mia firmly. 'I have to. If Bella is very sick I should be with her!'

'But what about going home?' Rory could see that Mia wasn't even listening to him. He couldn't let her go on her own – and what if Conrad was somehow involved in all of this?

'I'll come with you,' he said quietly.

Delighted, Mia squeezed his hand. 'You know we'll have to ride on the dragons, don't you?'

He tried not to think about it. The dragons stood patiently, waiting for them.

Mia pulled herself up on to Trig's back, the small dragon kept perfectly still. Excitement sparkled and fizzed inside her – this was something she'd dreamed of doing for such a long time. Rory walked warily towards Arznel, the black dragon was much bigger than he expected. It took three attempts before he managed to climb on to its back. There were no reins or straps of any kind to hang on to, so Rory grabbed a clump of leathery dragon skin, clinging on for dear life.

They lifted high into the air. Rory shut his eyes as Arznel, wings at full span, climbed higher and higher. The country-side fell away below them as brother and sister flew through the air on the dragons.

Looking down on Dragon Wood, Rory realised the true majesty of its ancient trees, their waving leaves tossed by the wind, sunlight painting them every shade of gold and green. They passed over Dwarf Vale, and Mia pointed out the various farms, and the winding ribbon of the river meandering far below them. Silver Lake, its deep waters sparkling with darting fish, glittered in the sunlight, the wind tossing and creasing the water as they flew over. Arznel was strong and carried Rory's weight easily, flying steadily through the wind. He was a good dragon, strong and true. Trig was smaller and at times seemed buffeted by pockets of wind. But the plucky little dragon kept on flying, and Mia eyes shone with delight and pride as she held on to him.

As they approached the stone turrets and ramparts of Blackwell Castle, the dragons began to circle, sinking lower and lower as the stone slabs of the courtyard came into view, each dragon gradually pulling in his wings and dropping his speed as he came in to land.

'That was the most wonderful, special thing that has ever happened to me!' Mia burst out, throwing her arms around Trig's neck and kissing him. The blue dragon looked equally adoringly at her.

Arznel stood perfectly still for Rory to dismount. The boy patted the dragon's neck, and stroked the side of his face.

'Thank you, Arznel ! I will never forget this day.'

The black dragon looked around, his green eyes meeting Rory's, and the boy knew that this had been a special day for both of them.

Crossing the courtyard, they approached the castle with trepidation.

Mia led the way through the Great Hall, past the banqueting room and down into the kitchen. Gwenda was not there, though a smell of baking filled the lower half of the castle.

'Come on! We'll try upstairs!' They took the stone steps two at a time. 'Where's Bella's room?'

Mia ran along the corridor ahead of her brother. She felt scared as she pushed open the door to the old woman's room. Bella lay in the large four-poster bed, a small shrunken figure, her long white hair spilling across the pillow.

'Is that you, child?'

Mia ran towards the dragon woman, flinging herself across the bed. 'I came back, Bella!' she sobbed.

'Don't cry, magician's daughter. I'm glad to see you! I knew if I sent Trig, he'd fetch you back.' The old woman patted her hand on the faded dragon coverlet. 'Sit by me, child'.

Mia clambered up beside Bella.

'I'm old ... much too old, and my time is running out ... none of us can live forever, no matter how powerful our magic is.'

Tears rolled down Mia's face.

'Don't cry, child! Are you crying for this wicked old witch who snatched you from your parents and carried you off? This sorceress who bewitched you and stole your childhood memories? This bad old Dragon Woman who shouted at you, and scolded you, and punished you, and made you work so hard and learn so much?'

Mia nodded, unable to speak, as tears welled in her eyes. The old woman held her close, and pressed her cheek to Mia's.

'The thing is, we understand each other, don't we, child? I

had to cross over into your world to find you. I took you from your family, your good parents and that grandmother of yours, and it was a wicked thing to do. I was thinking only of myself, and of the dragons and the world that could be yours, my young apprentice.' She stopped and looked feebly around the room. 'That brother of yours – is he here?'

Mia nodded.

Rory was standing at the bottom of the bed. Beside him stood Conrad.

'He is braver than most knights and dragon keepers of my acquaintance. Of course, I forgot that he too is a magician's son.'

Mia stroked the old woman's hand. It felt cold and she rubbed it again, trying to warm it.

'I was taken from my family when I was only five years of age and was reared with the dragons. Dracon – the Great Mage himself – made me his apprentice. I was much too young, of course. There was never time to get married or have a child, the magic was all that mattered. I have lived through many lifetimes, seen many great things, and always there has been deep magic and dragons. Their time is come again. The old ones in the wood are all dead and gone but these orphans – why, these are the finest dragons I have seen in many lifetimes! But they will need much protection and care, for always there are enemies.'

Bella was tiring herself with talking. Her breath became uneven and her voice weakened.

'I want to give you something, Mia. Gwenda will fetch it for you.'

Leaning against the piled-up pillows, the old woman began to cough, her eyes closed in pain.

'You must return to your mother. But Mia, you must remember that there is a place in both worlds for you and your brother. Gwenda has promised to look after the dragons in your absence and now that the Great Mage has returned, I know that the dragons will be protected.'

Conrad stepped forward and kissed Bella's hand. With tears in his eyes, he bowed his head to her.

Mia leaned forward, concentrating hard and trying to understand all that the old woman was telling her.

Bella drifted in and out of sleep, muttering to herself.

'Soon ... my time is running out ... lived far too long.'

Gradually, the old woman became peaceful, all care and worry left her worn features and she began to look beautiful, her face mirroring the face of the girl in the painting that hung across from her bed.

Mia hugged the old woman close. She willed life into her, silently begging Bella not to die. But slowly, breath and heart-beat and life ebbed from the ancient Dragon Woman, until finally she slept, never to wake again.

From outside in the castle's courtyard and across the lake, there rose a great noise – one by one, the dragons began to roar. Their mournful sound echoed all through the dark woods, the ancient cry of sorrow and loss.

Chapter 31

The Great Mage

Mia cried and cried after Bella's death. Rory, Conrad and Gwenda were unable to console her. All the people of Dwarf Vale and Dragon Wood came to pay their respects to Bella Blackwell, filing past the coffin that lay, guarded by two dragons, on the table in the Great Hall. Wizards and witches and magicians from all over remembered well the old woman they called 'the Great Sorceress.' Bella had asked to be buried in her beloved woods. The sad band of mourners carried out her final wishes.

Conrad had organised everything for the funeral ceremony, and when they returned to Blackwell Castle, Rory realised how well his friend had taken to running both the castle and the dragon school.

Conrad's jet-black hair hung loose about his shoulders and he wore a cloak of heavy purple velvet. He seemed different now, more than just a mere woodsman. But he was kindness itself to Mia and asked her to sit by him as they ate.

Mia's skin was pale and her eyes still red-rimmed and raw. Rory didn't know if he was imagining it or not, but a small freckle or stain had appeared on her cheek, in the shape of a wing – a dragon's wing.

'Conrad, what did Bella mean about the Great Mage returning?' asked Mia softly.

Conrad looked uncomfortable, toying with the food on his plate.

'Bella was talking about the most powerful magician of all, who controlled these lands and this world and, of course, the dragons.'

'Do you think that he is coming back, Conrad?'

Conrad nodded, his brown eyes serious as he answered Mia's questions.

'It is true, the old magic is born again,' agreed Conrad. 'You can sense it throughout the land. With the return of the dragons, the giants, dwarves and elves are all stirring too.'

'I will miss Bella so much', she said softly, 'but I think that she didn't mind dying because she knew that the Great Mage had already come and would take her place.'

Conrad stared into Mia's eyes. 'What are you saying?'

'I am saying that I have watched the dragons and how you speak to them, and how they understand what you want without you even having to say anything. I have seen how you know your way from one end of this castle to the other, and how Gwenda and the rest of the dwarves and elves bow down and respect you. And I know that you saved my brother's life and guarded him in the Wood and guided him safely to me.'

'For one so young, you have great wisdom, now I know why Bella chose you to be her apprentice,' replied Conrad dryly.

Rory had no idea what Mia was going on about. He didn't want his sister and his friend arguing and having a stupid fight.

'Are you the Great Mage, the mighty magician, the dragon keeper?' challenged Mia.

Conrad nodded. Rory couldn't believe it! He'd expected Conrad to throw back his head and laugh at Mia for saying such a ludicrous thing, to slap his thigh and make a joke, to stand up and protest and say Mia had got it all wrong. Instead, he sat there, nodding.

'Is it true?' demanded Rory, staring hard at his friend.

'Aye, it's true!' said Conrad, looking him straight in the eye.

'I knew it was you from the very first second I saw you!' smiled Mia triumphantly.

'I'm sorry Rory, I didn't mean to deceive you, but out there in Dragon Wood we met as equals and I was happy to join you on your quest. I knew that Bella had taken your sister. That was why I sent the Shadow Hound to bring you across into my world.'

'You brought me here!' said Rory angrily *'You* did!'

'Well, I played some part in it, but much of it you did your-self. Magic and the dragons have always been a part of my life, part of my destiny, and now they have become part of yours. With Bella's death it is now my turn to guard Dragon Wood and to ensure that these young dragons will be safe, and that there will always be a place in the world for ancient wisdom and deep magic,' explained Conrad.

Rory sat down, finally ready to listen.

'From the time of the great druids, my family has learned the lore of ancient magic and protected it,' explained Conrad. 'It was the great Dracon himself who decided to safeguard old magic and create a world where giants and dragons and dwarves and elves could all remain safe, protected from humans and from time.'

'I still don't understand,' murmured Mia 'Who is this Dracon? Was he your father, grandfather?'

'Dracon was, Dracon is, and Dracon will be,' said Conrad firmly, 'and now I am he.'

Rory still couldn't believe that Conrad was the all-powerful Great Mage and had been all along.

'But what about back in the woods? What were you doing there?'

'My friend Rory, all heroes must be challenged. You passed the test of courage and resolve well, as did your sister.'

'What about Bella?'

'Bella was one of the wisest magicians who ever lived. She devoted her life to the dragons. Dracon entrusted her with the dragon eggs and tiny orphan new-borns, and he knew she would protect and guard his dragons and their wood.'

'I wish she hadn't died,' said Mia softly.

'I know,' answered Conrad, 'but she has taught you much, even in a short time. Good lessons are never wasted.'

'We will have to return to our own world and our family soon,' insisted Rory. 'Though how we will get back now I'm not sure.'

'Bella left you a gift,' Conrad announced, 'it is time you received it!'

Gwenda appeared carrying a gold casket, which she placed on the floor in front of them.

'It was Bella's wish that you should have this, Mia.'

Mia raised the lid, gasping with surprise. It was the flying coat! There it lay, carefully folded, the multicoloured feathers flattened and dull, waiting for her to use it.

'It's mine! Look Rory, this is the coat I was telling you about! Do you know what this means?'

Pulling the coat from the casket to show her brother, she swirled it round her shoulders. The feathers filled out and changed colour.

At the bottom of the casket lay a second coat of a different hue. Gwenda, blushing with pride, pulled it out and placed it across Rory's shoulders.

'And this one is yours. Bella left it for you.'

Rory stood staring in disbelief. Imagine the old witch leaving him something too!

Conrad hugged him close.

'You and Mia are not my prisoners. You are free to come and

go as you please. Now, with these coats, you have no excuse, my friend!'

Mia looked at her brother. 'Are we going home, Rory?'

Rory nodded, not trusting himself to speak. 'Yes Mia!' he eventually stuttered, emotion choking him. 'We're going back to Glenkilty!'

Chapter 32

As Before ...

Rory and Mia rose early the next morning. Gwenda cooked an enormous breakfast and expected them to eat every last crumb. Rory's stomach was churning with excitement and nerves and poor Mia looked like she hadn't slept a wink all night. Rory did his best to eat heartily; he knew how much trouble the dwelf girl had taken to prepare the meal. Mia just picked at the scrambled eggs and nibbled half a potato cake.

As soon as breakfast was over, Mia jumped up from the table and ran upstairs, through the castle and out to the courtyards. Conrad was already there, working with the dragons in the early morning sunshine.

Mia went from one dragon to the other bidding each of them farewell. How had they grown so big in such a short time? She patted Arznel, the black dragon blowing hot air at her down his nose.

'You'll be blowing fire next, Arznel!' she joked, tickling him under the chin.

When Mia came to Rana, she noticed the tears in the dragon's eyes and stroked her very gently.

'Now, don't you go making me cry too!'

Dink, the boisterous green dragon, was his usual self and butted her with his snout, looking for attention.

'I promise I won't forget you either, Dink.'

Gosha nuzzled her, licking her hands, and Flett and Frezz pushed at each other trying to get closer to her.

'Now, no fighting!' she warned them, giving each of them a kiss on the snout.

Oro stood totally still with his head bent as Mia tickled his golden belly one last time.

Trig stood back from the rest and Mia went and wrapped her arms tightly around his neck. The blue dragon would always be her favourite. Trig hung his long neck and bent his head close to hers. Mia looked at Conrad who nodded at her, understanding the silent communication between dragon and master. In an instant the young girl was on Trig's back, and the dragon lifted from the grey stone courtyard, turned smoothly, and took off across the castle's ramparts, out into the morning sunshine.

Rory ran after them, a look of surprise on his face. Conrad held him back, as Trig and Mia flew skywards. Mia held on tightly as Trig circled smoothly, taking in the timeless beauty of Dragon Wood, Silver Lake, Dwarf Vale and Blackwell Castle. Mia was filled with joy as she flew with the dragon, her hair blowing in the wind. She would remember every second of that perfect dragon flight for the rest of her life.

Slowing down, Trig began to glide. Approaching the castle, his lonesome dragon roar broke the stillness of the morning air. As he landed, Mia knew that the strong bond between her and the blue dragon would forever remain unbroken.

'I'll return,' she whispered to him. Trig looked at her with mournful eyes.

'It is time to leave,' said Conrad. 'The sky is clear and there is a good strong breeze. You must both make ready!'

Rory and Mia put on their flying coats, making sure they were securely fastened. The coats fitted perfectly over their arms and legs.

'The coats are fine,' murmured Conrad. 'You must take good care of them and keep them in a safe, dry place. Remember that the feathers need to be used every so often or they will become stiff and useless.'

Mia stretched her feathered arms and pushed her hair off her face. Gwenda fussed over her like a mother hen, putting bread and sausage in her pocket in case she got hungry during the journey. How could Mia ever thank the dwelf girl for all her kindness? Rory and Conrad shook hands, respect and deep friendship in their eyes.

'I will miss you, brave Rory. Remember that you are a magician's son, too!' warned Conrad. 'No matter what you say or do, you can't change that!'

It was almost mid-morning by the time they eventually left the castle. Rory and Mia held hands, and stood with arms outstretched on the ledge of the main courtyard. Then they looked at each other nervously and jumped!

The feathers caught the wind and they could feel the muscles tighten in their arms as they began to fly. In only a few minutes, Conrad, Gwenda and the dragons fell away below them and disappeared from their sight.

Who could say how long they flew. At one point, a curious goose circled them, curious to know what type of birds they were, and a flock of gullion almost crashed into them and sent them off-course. Rory was pleased to see that the giants had made a start on the huge bridge that would span the swamp and eventually link the territories of Terra and Arbor.

The sun disappeared and it began to rain, but the waterproof feathers clung snugly to their bodies as the children flew on. Day changed to night and soon they only had the moon for company. Hour after hour Rory and Mia flew, until they were exhausted. They had to stop themselves falling asleep – the rhythmical sound and movement of the wings made them so drowsy!

Eventually, the darkness began to leave the sky and streaks of early light appeared on the horizon.

'How much further!' yawned Mia. 'My arms and legs hurt.'

Rory hadn't a clue, but he knew that the terrain had changed. It had become more familiar.

'Is that the church tower?'

The children felt a growing sense of excitement as they recognised familiar landmarks. After all, Conrad had said that everything at home in Glenkilty would be as they left it.

'There's Mulligan's farm!'

'Look Rory, there's our school!'

'There's the main street!'

All tiredness disappeared as they followed the curve of the winding road that led out past the lake. Far below stretched the giant trees of Glenkilty Wood. Mia could see the grey tiled roof and the tall chimney of their own house and the various greens of her mother's herbaceous border.

'We should land in the wood,' said Rory, 'in case anyone sees us.'

It was a difficult landing. Both children clipped the branches of trees and almost fell through the dense foliage to the ground. The magpies and rooks cawed in uproar at the two strange birds that had invaded their woods. Brushing themselves off and slightly shaken, Rory and Mia took off their feathered coats and folded them carefully.

'Where will we hide them?'

Rory looked around, searching for a suitable hiding place. He found a large, dry hole in the centre of a chestnut tree, and placed the flying coats carefully inside.

'We'll come back for them later!'

Mia felt nervous and the ground seemed to tilt and wobble beneath her feet as she and Rory walked towards home. What would their mum and dad say, how could they possibly explain their absence? They crossed over the back fence and pushed through the hedge. The back door stood wide open.

Jackie ran towards them, frantic with delight, barking madly, and flinging her small body at their feet, nearly tripping them up in the process. Mia gasped when she looked at the empty house next door. Trailing thick green ivy covered every brick and corner of the house and dusky pink roses clambered round every door and window, and by the front door was a huge bush of white and yellow daisies.

'Rory!' she gasped alarmed. Conrad had *promised* everything would be as it was before!

'Mia, just close your eyes and think of ... before!' urged Rory.

'Everything should be as before!' Mia chanted aloud, letting the image fill her head and feeling a swell of tingling magic ripple through her fingers and toes.

'Look!' shouted Rory in excitement. Before their eyes the house next door began to change. The ivy retreated as the roses shrivelled, and the white daisies disappeared into the grass. It was incredible! Suddenly, the hall door opened and Granny Rose and her two friends stumbled out.

'Oh, dear me!' groaned Daisy Donovan, 'I've a splitting headache.'

'What are you doing in there, Granny? Are you feeling all right?' asked Mia.

'Mia, child, there you are safe and well after giving us all such a fright!'

'It's all right Granny,' assured Rory. 'I told you I'd find her and bring her home.'

The three old women seemed slightly bewildered and confused.

'It was the strangest thing,' murmured Ivy Harrington, 'We came in to try and find you, Mia, and that nasty neighbour of yours, well, she put a spell on ...'

Rose Murphy nudged her best friend, giving her a warning glance. The three old woman looked at each other. Their twinkling old eyes met, and shared a silent secret.

Daisy and Ivy walked back to the Murphys' driveway, and climbed into their battered green mini. The children and their grandmother waved goodbye as they drove away.

Relieved, Rose Murphy hugged her grandchildren, wrapping her arms around them as they walked back across the lawn. 'Your Mum and Dad will be home in two days, then we'll all be back to normal. I'll not ask you two where you've been,' smiled their Granny, fixing her gaze on them. 'I'm much too old and much too wise to do that. All I'll say is, I'm glad you're back!

Mia turned back towards the witch's house. It was empty now. Tears filled her eyes when she remembered Bella, the old Dragon Woman, and the good and bad times they had shared. The great sorceress's *Olde Magick* book was tucked safely under her arm, for there was much a young apprentice needed to learn if she wanted to be a great magician...

OTHER BOOKS BY MARITA CONLON-McKENNA

UNDER THE HAWTHORN TREE
Winner International Reading Association Award;
Reading Association of Ireland Award

Ireland in the 1840s is devastated by famine. When tragedy strikes their family, Eily, Michael and Peggy are left to fend for themselves. Starving and in danger of ending up in the dreaded workhouse, they escape. Their one hope is to find the great-aunts they have heard about in their mother's stories.

WILDFLOWER GIRL
Winner Bisto Merit Award – Historical Fiction

Peggy, from *Under the Hawthorn Tree*, is now thirteen and must leave Ireland for America. After a terrible journey on board ship, she arrives in Boston. What kind of life will she find there?

FIELDS OF HOME

In Ireland, Eily and her family struggle to make a living on a small farm. Michael works with horses at the Big House, while in America, Peggy hears the call of the wild west. Will the family ever be together again?

www.obrien.ie